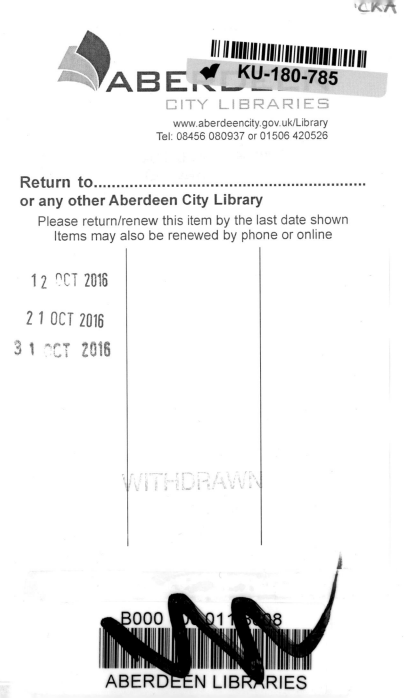

Rachel bent down and picked his wallet up without thinking. It was an expensive wallet. Black leather with fine stitching. Like something her father would own.

Her eyes skimmed over to his ID. He had an American driver's license. Which seemed odd. Because he was Greek, no question.

Okay, snoopy. Not really your business.

And it wasn't. They weren't trading life stories so it wasn't really fair for her to be looking at his personal property.

Before she could snap the wallet shut and put it on the table she read his name. Not on purpose. But she saw it, and then all she could do was stare.

She knew his name.

And for a full thirty seconds she didn't know from where.

Alexios Christofides.

She heard the name in Ajax's voice. A growl, a curse.

He wasn't a stranger.

She'd been seduced by her fiancé's enemy.

Maisey Yates was an avid Mills & Boon® Modern™ Romance reader before she began to write them. She still can't quite believe she's lucky enough to get to create her very own sexy alpha heroes and feisty heroines. Seeing her name on one of those lovely covers is a dream come true.

Maisey lives with her handsome, wonderful, diaper-changing husband and three small children across the street from her extremely supportive parents and the home she grew up in, in the wilds of Southern Oregon, USA. She enjoys the contrast of living in a place where you might wake up to find a bear on your back porch and then heading into the home office to write stories that take place in exotic urban locales.

Recent titles by the same author:

PRETENDER TO THE THRONE
  (The Call of Duty)
FORGED IN THE DESERT HEAT
A HUNGER FOR THE FORBIDDEN
HIS RING IS NOT ENOUGH

**Did you know these are also available as eBooks?
Visit www.millsandboon.co.uk**

ONE NIGHT TO RISK IT ALL

BY
MAISEY YATES

Published in Great Britain 2014
by Mills & Boon, an imprint of Harlequin (UK) Limited,
Eton House, 18-24 Paradise Road, Richmond, Surrey, TW9 1SR

© 2014 Maisey Yates

ISBN: 978 0 263 24218 8

Harlequin (UK) Limited's policy is to use papers that are natural,
renewable and recyclable products and made from wood grown in
sustainable forests. The logging and manufacturing processes conform
to the legal environmental regulations of the country of origin.

Printed and bound in Great Britain
by CPI Antony Rowe, Chippenham, Wiltshire

B ooo ooo oll 8608

ONE NIGHT TO RISK IT ALL

To my family.

Because it takes a village to support me, and you all do it with remarkable ease, very little grumbling, and a lot of love.

You can never know how much I appreciate you.

CHAPTER ONE

RACHEL HOLT'S FOCUS was pulled to the nightstand. To the ring glittering there in the bedside table light. She lifted her left hand and looked at the finger the ring had been on only a few hours ago.

Strange to see it bare after so much time wearing it.

But it hadn't seemed right to wear it now.

She picked it up off the nightstand and held it up, watching it sparkle, then turned over and looked at the man sleeping next to her. His arm thrown up over his head, his eyes closed, dark curls falling into his face. He was like an angel. A wonderful fallen angel who'd shown her some deliciously sinful things.

But he wasn't the man who'd given her the ring. He wasn't the man she was supposed to marry next month.

That was a problem.

He was so beautiful, though, it was hard to think of him as a problem. Alex, with the beautiful deep blue eyes and golden-brown skin. Alex, whom she'd met that afternoon—oh, good Lord, she'd known him less than twenty-four hours—on the docks.

She looked at the clock. She'd known him for eight hours. Eight hours had been all it took for her to shed years of staid, respectable behavior. To shed her engagement ring, and follow her… She couldn't say heart. It was hormones, clearly.

What had she been thinking? It hadn't been anything like the way she normally behaved. Not at all. She knew better than this. Knew better than to let emotion or passion overcome common sense and decorum.

There had been no decorum tonight.

From the first moment she'd seen him, she'd been completely captivated by the way he moved. The way his muscles shifted as he worked at cleaning the deck.

She closed her eyes and went straight back there. And it was easy to remember what had made her lose her mind... and her clothes.

It was the most beautiful weather they'd had since they'd arrived in Corfu. Not too hot, a breeze blowing in off the sea. Rachel and Alana had just finished lunch, and her friend was headed to the airport to fly back to New York, while Rachel was staying on to represent the Holt family at a charity event.

This vacation was her last hurrah before her wedding next month. A sowing of oats, in a respectable manner of course, as anyone would want to do before they tied themselves, body and soul, to another person for the rest of their lives.

"More shoes?" Alana asked, gesturing to the little boutique shop that was just across the pale, stone street.

"I'm going to say no," Rachel said, looking out across the water, at the ships, the yachts, that were tethered to the docks.

"Are you sick?"

She laughed and walked over to the seawall, bracing herself on it. "Maybe."

"It's the wedding, isn't it?" Alana asked.

"It shouldn't be. I've known it was coming for ages. We've had an understanding for six years and been engaged for a good portion of those years. The date for the wedding has been set for almost eleven months. So…"

"You're allowed to change your mind," Alana said.

"No. I'm not. I… Can you imagine? The wedding is the social event of the year. Jax is finally going to get Holt. My father will finally have him as a son, which we all know is what both of them want."

"What about what *you* want?"

It had been so long since she'd asked herself that question, she honestly didn't know the answer.

"I…care about Ajax."

"Do you love him?"

Her eye caught movement out on one of the yachts—a man was on the deck cleaning. He was shirtless, a pair of loose, faded shorts clinging to lean hips. Aided by the sun, the light clinging to the ridges of muscle, the shadow settling in the hollows, she could clearly see the defined, cut lines of his body.

And he took her breath away.

In one moment she had all of the passion, all of the heat, all of the deep longing she'd been growing so certain she was missing—sucked out of her by that horrendous early heartbreak—sweep through her like a wave.

"No," she said, her eyes never leaving the man on the yacht, "no, I don't love him. Not—not like you mean. I'm not in love with him. I *do* love him, it's just not…that kind."

It wasn't a revelation. But coming on the heels of that sudden rush of sensation, it was more disturbing than normal.

She'd sort of thought that maybe it was her fault. Not her and Ajax together, but just the way they were as people. Ajax wasn't a passionate man, and he never demonstrated passion with her. Quite the contrary, he barely touched her. After all their years together he never went further than a kiss. A nice, deep kiss sometimes. Sometimes a kiss that lasted a long while on the couch in his penthouse. But no clothes were ever shed. The earth was never shattered. It was never hard to stop.

And because he was a very handsome man, she'd assumed that the problem—if it could be called a problem—was with both of them. That she was missing a piece of herself, passion choked out after years of tight control. After letting her passion carry her to the edge of a cliff all those years ago, only to be pulled back just in time, so very aware of the fate she'd been saved from.

Since then, she'd kept it on a tight leash. Which made them sort of an ideal couple, in her mind.

But that wasn't true. She knew it now. In a blinding flash of clarity, she knew it.

She had passion. It was still there. And she *wanted*.

"What are you going to do?" Alana asked, sounding heavily concerned now.

Rachel's face heated. "Um…about?"

"You don't love him."

Oh. Of course Alana wasn't in her head—she didn't know that Rachel's world had just been rocked by a man more than one hundred yards away.

She waved a hand. "Yes, but that's nothing new to me."

"You're staring at that man over there."

Rachel blinked. "Am I?"

"Obviously."

"Well he's…"

"Mmm. Yes, he is. Go talk to him."

"What?" Rachel whipped around to look at Alana. "Just…go talk to him?"

"Yeah. I don't have to get on my plane for another few hours so if you need a bailout, I'm here. But I can hang back."

"Go talk to him and what?"

Flirtation, living dangerously, living for the moment—

that was all a part of a past so long gone it felt like it belonged to someone else entirely. The Rachel who had narrowly escaped humiliating herself and her family was gone. New Rachel had emerged from the wreckage. And New Rachel was a rule follower. A peacekeeper. She went with the flow and did what she could to keep everyone happy. To make sure she didn't go too far over the line and miss the safety net her father provided for her.

But for some reason, standing there in the sunshine, thinking of the safety her father provided, of the stability she had with Ajax, she felt like she was drowning in the air. Felt like there was a noose tightening around her neck, the countdown to her execution looming....

Such drama, Rachel, it's a wedding, not a hanging.

But even so, she felt like it was. Because the wedding presented her with utter, final certainty for her future. A future as Ajax's wife. As New Rachel, the one who never created a ripple on the surface, for the rest of her life.

"You have got to go and talk to him," Alana said. "You turned red when you first saw him. Like...really red. Like he lit your toes on fire."

Rachel choked. "Dramatic much?"

"So okay, I've sat back and watched your engagement with Ajax, and I haven't said much. But as you just said, you aren't madly in love with him. And anyone with eyes sees that."

"I know," she said, her throat tightening.

"Look, I know we're old and boring now. And I know that in high school we did some stupid stuff...."

"To say the least," Rachel said.

Alana continued. "But I think you've gone a little bit too far the other way."

"The alternative wasn't any good."

"Maybe not. But I think maybe this future isn't so good, either."

"What else can I do, Alana?" Rachel asked. "My dad bailed me out so many times, and I pushed him to the point where he was ready to wash his hands of me. And now? We're close. We have a relationship. I make him proud. And if Ajax is the price I have to pay for that then…I accept it."

"Does he at least make you feel like your toes have been lit on fire?"

Rachel looked at the man on the yacht again. "No," she said, the word choked out. "He doesn't."

"Then I think you owe it to yourself to spend some time with a man who does."

"Really?"

"Yes, really. I really do."

"So…I should just go talk to him? Want to bet he curses me out in Greek and then goes back to work?"

Alana laughed. "Yeah, that won't happen, Rach."

"How do you know? Maybe he doesn't like blondes."

"He'll like you because you're the kind of woman who drives men crazy."

"Not so much anymore." Flirting, toying and teasing had ended badly for her eleven years ago, and Ajax had certainly never acted as if she'd driven him crazy.

"Lies," Alana said, waving her hand. "Live dangerously for a minute, babe. Before you stop living altogether."

Rachel couldn't take her eyes off him, not even to shoot her friend the evil eye, which is what she should really be doing. "Did you read that on a fortune cookie?"

"Ever had an orgasm with an actual man? 'Cause I have. So…"

At the mention of orgasms, Rachel's cheeks burned. No, no she hadn't. She'd given them a few times, yes, but never received. "Fine. I'll go talk to him," she said. "Talk to. Not orgasm with. Lower that suggestive eyebrow of yours."

"Okay. And I'll be close. So if you…you know, need anything, text."

"Also I have mace," Rachel said. "Ajax insisted."

She winced as she mentioned her fiancé's name. But she wasn't going to do anything, not really. She was just going to go talk to Shirtless Sailor Stud. She wasn't going to do anything inappropriate.

It was all about having a moment. Just a moment. To be brave and reckless, and not so much like the Rachel she'd been this past decade. To know what it was like to chase a moment that wasn't bound up in the expectations of other people.

Just a moment. To talk to a guy because she thought he was cute. Nothing more.

She took a breath and tossed her hair over her shoulder. "Wish me…well, not luck exactly."

Alana winked. "Get lucky."

"No. I'm not cheating on Jax."

"Okay," Alana said.

"I'm *not*." The very idea was laughable. There were people who were like that. Bold people who went around *carpe*-ing *diems* all over the place. But that wasn't her. Not anymore. She wasn't sure that had ever been her. Her rebellious years had been just that. Rebellion. Not just a desire for freedom, but a desire to push against the bonds that had always held her in place. Until she'd realized just how much that behavior affected other people. Just how much it could affect her. Not just her present, but her entire future.

But just saying hi wasn't so bad. There was no harm in giving herself a moment to bask in the heat that this stranger gave off.

"Riiiight," Alana said.

"Shush." Rachel turned and walked toward the dock, her hands shaking, her body rebelling in every way against what she was about to do. Sweaty palms, heart beating so fast she was pretty sure she was going to faint, mouth watering with sickness. Yep, the signs to run and preserve herself were all there.

But she ignored them.

She looked back at Alana one more time, who was standing at the wall still, watching. Then she turned back to her target.

She would just say hi. And maybe flirt. Just a little harmless flirting. She half remembered how that went. She'd been a master of the tease back in the day. Batting her eyes and touching a guy's shoulder, all while never intending to do anything more than use his interest to boost her ego. It had been a game then. Fun.

Why not revisit it? This was her last hurrah before her marriage. A chance to hang and shop with Alana. A little time to decompress, loll by the beach, watch chick flicks in her hotel room, then enjoy a charity gala. All without her family or Ajax around.

This was just a part of that. A little time off from being Rachel Holt, beloved media figure. Rachel Holt, who was doing her best to represent her family, to do what was right.

She needed some time to just be Rachel. Not New Rachel. Not Old Rachel, either. Just Rachel.

She stopped in front of the yacht and took a deep breath that was choked off.

Then she looked up, and her gaze crashed into the most electric blue eyes she'd ever seen. Followed by a slow, wicked smile, a flash of bright white teeth on dark skin. He was even more beautiful up close. Utterly arresting. He pushed dark curls out of his eyes and the motion made his muscles flex. A show just for her. And her hormones stood and applauded. And cheered for an encore.

Stupid hormones.

"Are you lost?" he asked, his English heavily accented. The same accent as Ajax's. Greek. And yet it didn't sound the same. It wasn't as refined. It had a rough edge that abraded against something deep inside her. Struck against the hard, dry places inside of her and set off a shower of sparks that sat smoldering, building.

And all that over three words. She was doomed if she did anything other than walk away.

But she didn't. She stayed rooted to the spot.

"Um…I was…I was just there," she gestured back to the wall where she'd been standing with Alana, who was now absent. "And I saw you."

"You saw me?"

"Yes."

"Was there a problem?"

"I…" she said, stumbling over her words. "Not a problem, no. I just noticed you."

"Is that all?"

He put his foot up on the metal railing that surrounded the deck then jumped down onto the dock, the motion fluid, shocking and…darn hot.

"Yes," she said. "That's all."

"Your name?"

"Rachel Holt."

She waited. For recognition to flash through his eyes. For him to get excited at being in front of someone who had a certain level of media fame. Or for him to turn away. People did one of those two things. Rarely anything else.

But there was no recognition. Nothing.

"Well, Rachel," he said, that voice a rush of liquid that pooled low in her body, "what is it you noticed about me?"

"That, um…you were hot," she said. She'd never been so forward with a man in her life. Though, honestly, she wasn't sure if she was being forward or being an idiot. She was good with people. The consummate hostess. Everyone, even the vicious press, liked her. A reputation that had been carefully cultivated—and fiercely guarded.

But she was a lot more experienced at offering people cold beverages than she was at offering them her body.

He arched one dark brow. "That I was hot?"

"Yeah. Haven't you ever had a woman come on to you before?" Her face was burning and she couldn't blame the afternoon sun. She wasn't supposed to be hitting on him, and yet these were the words leaving her mouth.

Stupid mouth. Almost as stupid as her hormones.

"Yes, but not in quite such a charming way. Did you have an end goal in mind for this?"

"I thought..." Suddenly she did. Suddenly she wanted everything, all at once, with this stranger. Wanted to touch him, kiss him, feel his fingertips forge a trail of fire over her bare skin as he took her to levels of ecstasy she'd never believed were possible for her to want, let alone feel. "I thought we could have a drink." A drink. A cold beverage. That was back in her comfort zone and maybe a bit smarter. Especially since she didn't even know his name. "What's your name?" she asked, because since she was engaging in naked fantasies about the man, it seemed polite to ask.

"Alex," he said.

"Just Alex?" she asked.

He lifted a shoulder, the muscles in his chest shifting with the motion. "Why not?"

Why not, indeed? It wasn't as though there was any reason for him to be anything else. Who cared what his last name was? She'd never have occasion to use it. She'd never introduce him at a party, or need to refer to him in conversation. She'd never see him after today.

"Good point. So, a drink? Or...would your boss get mad?"

"My boss?"

"The owner of the yacht."

He frowned and looked behind him, then back at her. "Oh. No, he's gone up to Athens for a few days. I'm just supposed to check in on things now and again. No need to stay tied to the dock."

"I suppose not. You won't float away." She laughed, then felt immediately stupid. Like she'd regressed to being an eighteen-year-old girl rather than a twenty-eight-year-old woman. Of course, she hadn't been giggly or ridiculous over men at eighteen. She'd learned better by then.

Apparently all good sense and life lessons were out the window now.

He wrinkled his nose and squinted against the sun, an oddly boyish gesture. It made her feel even warmer. "I don't suppose. Though I have in the past."

"Have you?"

"Sure. That's how I ended up here. I spend a lot of my life floating."

She felt the layered meaning in his words. And in a strange way, felt like she'd heard more honest words from this stranger, this man she'd known all of five minutes, than she'd ever heard out of the man she was planning to marry.

"So," he said, "drink?"

"Of course."

"Let me just get a shirt." He tossed her a smile and climbed back up onto the boat. It took all of her willpower not to say "oh, no, please leave your chest bare." She figured that would be pushing it. Especially since, no matter how much she might want him, she knew she'd never do anything about it.

A drink was all it would ever be.

They'd gone to the bar next and ordered a couple of sodas. She'd texted Alana to let her know everything was fine and that she wasn't axe-murdered. But she didn't send a text when she and Alex walked around town for hours, or when they ended up having dinner on the pier, laughing and talking over seafood and pasta. She didn't text Alana about how he lifted his fork to her lips and let her taste his entrée, about the way their eyes had met in that moment and it had sent a snap of heat through her.

Or when he took her to a club later that night.

She hadn't been to a club since she'd had to sneak in with a fake ID. Clubs like this were a hotbed of scandal and sex, and all sorts of things her father and Ajax would never have approved of. The sort of place the press would crucify her for going to.

Alcohol, loud thumping music, sticky dance floors filled with bodies. There had been a time when she'd loved it. But not after she'd become aware of what she was inviting. Not since she realized the sort of trouble she could get herself into. Since she realized she'd been walking down a path that only had one ending, and it wasn't a happy one.

But just for now, she was going to put good behavior on hold. She felt secluded here, insulated by whatever magic spell Alex had cast on her the first moment she'd seen him. No one around was looking at her, expecting her to behave in a certain way. She didn't think she was in any danger of exposing herself the way she'd done in the past.

Somehow, with Alex, it felt exciting. It felt dangerous— a hit of adrenaline she used to crave. One she'd denied herself for far too long.

It all did. The whole day. It was like being on a vacation from herself, and she loved it. Or maybe it was a vacation *to* herself, but that was a step further into the philosophical than she wanted to get.

"This is so fun!" she shouted, trying to make her voice heard over the thumping bass.

"You are enjoying yourself?" he asked.

"Very."

He took her left hand and the touch of his skin against hers sent a lightning bolt shooting from her wrist to her core. "I have been meaning to ask about this," he said, tilting her knuckles so that her engagement ring caught the light.

Looking at it made her stomach crash into her toes. She didn't want to think about that. About reality. Not at all.

"I'm not married," she said.

A wicked smile curved his lips, blue eyes glittering in the dim light. "I wouldn't have cared if you were. I would have maybe just asked how big your husband was. And if he was connected to organized crime in any way."

The thought of Ajax being connected to anything as sordid or exciting as organized crime was hysterically funny. He was far too staid for anything that outrageous. He was the calming, steadying influence in her life. Or at least that's how her father saw him. And she couldn't really imagine him mustering up any rage for Alex being here at the club with her.

Ajax wasn't really a club kind of guy. If she'd asked him, he would have probably waved his hands and said to have fun while he went back to sorting numbers into columns or whatever it was he did all night in his office that gave him such satisfaction.

"Um…you don't need to be concerned. Besides, we haven't done anything we should be ashamed of," she said. "I haven't…violated any vows."

"Yet," he said, his grin turning wicked. "It's still early."

"So it is," she said, her heart thundering hard.

"Do you want to dance?"

She looked at his outstretched hand and she felt an ache, a need, tighten in her belly. Ajax had never once danced with her. Had never even asked. And until that moment, she hadn't realized that she'd been missing it.

In that same moment, she realized that this wasn't just a request for a simple dance.

She knew that this was it. The deciding moment. That

if she said yes to this, she wouldn't say no again for the rest of the night.

But maybe that had been true hours ago. Maybe from the moment she'd locked eyes with him, saying no had been an impossibility.

"Yes," she said, the word torn from her, scraping her throat raw and leaving in its place a sweet, light relief. She had decided. Tonight she was going to embrace life, whatever that meant. "Yes, Alex, I want to dance."

CHAPTER TWO

HE KISSED HER for the first time out on the dance floor. There were people all around them, the crush of bodies intense. And she let them push her into him, let them drive her against him so that she could feel the hard heat of his muscles against her chest.

When she was pressed against him, she looked up, angled her head toward his. She knew she was begging for it and she didn't care. Because she needed this. More than air. It didn't matter what happened tomorrow, or in the month leading up to her wedding, not if she didn't survive this night.

And it felt like she might not if he didn't touch her. If she couldn't taste him.

But he didn't make her beg for long.

He dipped his head and claimed her mouth, his tongue forcing her lips apart. She opened to him, took him in deep, kissed him until she was dizzy. There had never been a kiss like this. Not for her, maybe not for anyone. One that stole her every thought, her every worry. One that reduced her to nothing more than need, nothing more than a deep, physical ache that demanded satisfaction.

She wrapped her arms around his neck and clung to him, her body moving against his, no longer in rhythm with the music, but in rhythm with her own desire. She forked her fingers through his thick, curly hair, held him against her, poured all of herself, all of the desire that had been building in her for so many years, into a kiss that she shouldn't be having. A kiss that was forbidden to her.

And that just made her angry. More determined to get what she needed tonight. What she would never have after tonight. This was her last chance.

A secret thrill. A secret bit of adventure. No one ever had to know.

"Come back to my hotel with me," she said, against his mouth, unable to part from him for even a second.

He didn't answer—he only kissed her again, and she realized there was no way he'd heard her, not over the music.

She pulled his head down and put her lips against his ear. "I have a hotel room. Come back with me."

That was all the encouragement he needed. Faster than she could change gears, Alex was dragging her off the dance floor and out into the warm summer night. He paused outside the club door, pushed her against the wall and kissed her, the motion and the kiss savage, explosive. Perfect. She arched into him, rubbing her breasts against the hard wall of his chest, trying to find some satisfaction for the need that was tearing through her like a beast.

"Now," she said, her eyes closed tight. "We have to go back now. I need… I can't…"

"I agree."

"It's close. I think it's close. I'm dizzy, actually. The city is sideways. It's hard to tell where the hell we are."

Alex laughed and pressed his forehead against hers. "I know exactly where the hell I am."

"And where is that?"

"With you. I don't need to know anything more."

She exhaled sharply, tried to ignore the stab of emotion in her chest. This wasn't supposed to make her feel. "Wow. You do say the best things. You really do."

He took her hand. "Lead the way."

She did. And somehow, right then, she felt more like herself than she ever had. Like the two halves of her life, the woman she was in public and the woman she was in private had merged together for the first time.

She felt brave. She felt certain.

She felt happy.

A whisper of who she'd been before she'd learned to shut herself down. Before the Colin debacle. And blackmail. Before she'd had to face her father and tell him what she'd done. And what the fallout from it might be.

I can't protect you anymore, Rachel. These choices you're making are dangerous. People, men, will always try to take advantage of you because of your connections, the press will always hunt you because of who you are, and you're courting it. No more. If you keep on like this, I will not cover for you again. I love you too much to enable you this way.

And less kind words from her mother. *A woman in your position can't afford these mistakes. It's not only immoral, it's dangerous. Think of what the press will say. About you. Us. I haven't spent all these years helping propel us to this position in society to watch you tear it down with stupid behavior!*

Angry words spoken in private. A side of her mother only Rachel ever saw.

But she'd taken those words, balled them up and stored them in her chest, kept them close, ever since.

Except…except this moment.

But it was different. It was out of time, out of the real world entirely. And Alex didn't even know who she was. He didn't want to use her. Didn't want to get her into a compromising position so he could sell photographs, or a dirty video.

Even Ajax, one of the kindest people she knew, wanted her for her name more than anything else.

But that wasn't Alex. Alex just wanted her.

That simple thought pushed everything dark away from her mind. Everything in the past, everything in the future. There was just now. And now was perfect.

They started walking down the sidewalk, then they were running, laughing. She bent and kicked her shoes off, carrying them in her free hand as she ran barefoot down the stone walk.

They stopped in front of the hotel, the lights from the lobby casting a glow on Alex, on the fountains in front of the building. "Oh, yes," she said, breathing heavily. "I'm in a nice hotel."

"So you are." He laughed, the sound reverberating through her body.

"Don't feel awkward or anything."

"I don't," he said.

Of course he wouldn't. It was hard to imagine him feeling awkward anywhere. "Good. I need to know at least three more things about you before we go in, okay?"

"Depends. Are you going to do a credit check?"

"I swear not," she said, "I won't even fingerprint you. But…you're a stranger, and I can't have that."

"Really? And what is it that will make me not a stranger?"

She squeezed her eyes shut for a moment, and when she opened them, Alex filled her visions. "Favorite color?"

"Don't have one."

"Come on. What color is your bedspread?"

He laughed. "Black."

"Okay. How old are you?"

"Twenty-six," he said.

"Oh." For some reason the answer sent a little thrill through her. "Well, I'm twenty-eight, I hope that doesn't deter you."

"Not in the least," he said. "I might, in fact, be more turned on now. If such a thing is possible."

Her pulse kicked into a higher gear. "One more thing," she said. "Would you rather…sleep under the stars, or in a beautiful suite?"

"Either. As long as you were with me. Preferably in a state of undress."

The air rushed out of her lungs. "Well, that was the perfect answer."

"Can we go in?"

"Yes," she said, of course, since there was no way she was saying no now. "You aren't a stranger now, so it's all good."

"I'm glad," he said.

They went into the hotel and passed quickly through the lobby. She pushed the button and stood in front of the elevator, waiting, her nerves building as each second ticked by.

As soon as they were inside, as soon as the doors closed behind them, he pushed her back against the wall, his mouth hungry on hers, his hands roaming over her curves.

She could feel the hard press of his erection against her hip, could feel his arousal, not just there, but in every line of his body. The tense hold of his shoulders, the thundering of his heart, the urgency in his kiss.

She'd never in her wildest fantasies imagined herself here. Like this. With a man kissing her like he was starving for her. She never imagined she would be kissing a man as though she was starving for him, in truth.

Her past experiences included fizzy, alcohol-flavored kisses and heavy coercion. This wasn't alcohol going to her head. Nor was it coerced. It wasn't about rebelling against her neat and orderly life. It wasn't about a sense of duty. It was about her.

They were at her floor not nearly fast enough and all too quickly. Any slower, she might have died—or he might have just taken her straight to heaven with her clothes on. She was close, so close, and she knew it.

She might not have ever considered herself overly passionate but she had a sex drive. And since Ajax was patiently waiting to take things to the next level, that meant she was an expert at satisfying that sex drive on her own.

Orgasm she knew. But having it entirely out of her control? That was a whole different matter. She'd given Colin pleasure, but he'd never really touched her. And anyway, that was eleven years ago, and the extent of her experience with men and any sort of nudity.

Now she was here, and Alex was definitely touching. And her pleasure was all in his control. It was both exhilarating and terrifying.

She walked out of the elevator into the hall, her legs shaking. She dug through her purse, trying to find the little key card she'd thrown in there earlier. Why had she been so careless? She hadn't had this in mind, that's for sure. She hadn't known there would be urgency. She had all the urgency and no flipping key....

She scraped the bottom of her purse with her hand and came up with the card. "Oh, thank God," she breathed. "That was sacrilege, wasn't it?" she asked, looking back at Alex.

"Why?"

"Thanking God because I found the key so we could... well, this is fornication, isn't it?"

"It will be in five minutes," he said. "Right now it's just lust."

"Pretty powerful stuff." She turned to the door and slid the key in the slot. The light turned green. "So, I guess we go in now."

He stopped and touched her cheek with the tip of his finger, the gesture so tender it shocked her. "You're very pretty when you're nervous."

Her face heated. "Well, that's nice of you to say."

His blue eyes locked with hers, so sincere, so focused. As if he could only see her, as if she was the only thing that mattered. No one had ever looked at her like that, not ever. "I mean it."

She coughed, her throat suddenly tight with emotion. "Well…thank you. But I'm less nervous when you kiss me. Maybe we should go with that?"

He didn't have to be asked twice.

He pulled her into the room and onto the bed. She was flat on her back, the mattress soft beneath her, Alex hard over her. She didn't have time to be nervous. She was too turned on, too in the moment.

There was nothing boyish about him now. The humorous light in his eyes was gone, replaced with something dark, feral. Dangerous.

And she liked it.

"I will be slow the next time," he said. "I promise. I like foreplay." He rose up onto his knees and stripped off his shirt. "And there will be some. Next time. Next time, I promise." Then he reached into his shorts pocket and took out his wallet, pulling out a condom and throwing the wallet down onto the floor, followed quickly by the rest of his clothes.

She didn't have time to be nervous—she was too busy looking at him. He was incredible, so much more than she'd imagined a man might be.

And she wanted… She just *wanted*.

He tugged the top of her dress down, bared her to him, lowered his head and sucked one nipple deep in his mouth as he pushed her skirt up over her hips.

He hooked his fingers into the sides of her panties and tugged them down her legs, then drew back for a moment, opening the condom and rolling it on quickly before he positioned himself between her thighs.

He put his hand beneath her bottom and tilted her up to him as he thrust deep inside her. She winced against the pain, fighting the urge to make a sound. Because she didn't want to ruin the moment. Even with the pain it was the most beautiful moment ever. The most exciting and wild thing that had ever happened to her.

It was perfect.

If he noticed, he had no reaction. And she was glad. Instead, he thrust deep inside of her, pushing them both higher and higher until she was gasping. Until she was fisting his hair, the sheets, whatever she could get hold of so she didn't fly off the bed and shatter into a million pieces.

The pain faded quickly, every thrust pushing her closer to the point of release. But it wasn't an easy push. It wasn't a gentle journey to the peak. It was fire and thunder—her release almost ripped from her as it hit, suddenly and before she could take a chance to breathe.

She shuddered out her release, clinging to his shoulders, legs wrapped around his calves. She was sure her nails were biting into his skin, but she didn't care. She couldn't.

He went still above her, a hoarse sound on his lips as he found his own pleasure. And then he was up, moving away from her and into the bathroom.

She lay there on her back, her dress pulled down over her breasts and up past her hips, trying to catch her breath, hands over her eyes. "Oh, dear Lord, what have I done?"

He came back in, the condom managed, the look on his face grim. "Now, you should have told me *that*," he said.

"Told you what?" she asked, sitting up and trying to put her dress in place. Though he didn't seem concerned with his nudity at all.

"That you were a virgin."

"Oh. That. Well. I *could* have told you. It's just that…"

"Just that what?"

"I didn't want to. How stupid is that?"

He walked over to the bed and took her left hand in his, holding it up so she was eye level with her engagement ring. "Whoever gave you this? He's an idiot."

Rachel came back to the present, her eyes on the ring, just like they'd been in that moment after her first time with Alex.

They'd been together at least four times in the hours since then. And he'd been telling the truth. He did like foreplay. Not only that, he was good at it. Darn good.

She put the ring back down, a smile curving her lips.

She sat up slowly, the muscles in her body complaining. Alex had given her a little bit more exercise than she was used to. That made her smile widen. Which was stupid, maybe, but she felt…different. Giddy. Alive.

Half in love.

She closed her eyes. No. She didn't want that. That was such a stupid cliché. She didn't actually know the man. She'd been naked with him, that was all.

Except it was easy to remember how it was to dance with him. How it felt to hold his hand as she walked barefoot down a city sidewalk. How she'd been different with him. More alive.

Happy.

So maybe it wasn't so stupid that she felt half in love. It was scary, though. She'd been…not in love, but infatuated with a guy before, with hideous results. But that had been different. It felt like another lifetime. Like it had happened to another girl.

She'd changed over the past eleven years. In ways that were necessary, but in ways that had left her feeling like she was trapped in skin that had become far too small.

And sometime last night, she'd changed again.

She got out of bed and stumbled to the bathroom, taking care of early morning necessities and looking at herself in the mirror. She looked… Her hair was a wreck. She was pretty sure the dark mark on her neck was a hickey.

She smiled. She should not be enjoying this. But she was.

Real life could be dealt with later.

She pushed her hair back and walked out into the hotel room again, and stopped when she saw Alex's wallet on the floor. It was open, from when he'd taken out the condom and thrown it onto the ground. After that incident, he'd procured protection from the concierge. Much to her chagrin.

Well, and delight, if she was completely honest. She'd absolutely benefitted from the acquisition of a box of condoms.

She bent down and picked his wallet up without thinking. It was an expensive wallet. Black leather with fine stitching. Like something her father, or Ajax, would own. Strange because his clothes were so worn. Because he worked on a boat.

Her eyes skimmed over to his ID. He had an American driver's license. Which seemed odd. Because he was Greek, no question. Though, perhaps his employer was American.

Okay, snoopy. Not really your business.

And it wasn't. They weren't trading life stories so it wasn't really fair for her to be looking at his personal property.

Before she could snap the wallet shut and put it on the table, she read his name. Not on purpose. But she saw it, and then all she could do was stare.

She knew his name.

And for a full thirty seconds, she didn't know from where.

Alexios Christofides.

She heard the name in Ajax's voice. A growl, a curse. He'd been nettling Ajax for months. Buying shares in his business, reporting him to the IRS for suspected tax wrongdoing, reporting him to environmental agencies. All false accusations, but things that had cost time and money.

He wasn't a cabin boy, that was for sure.

And he wasn't a stranger.

She'd been seduced by her fiancé's enemy.

She thought the floor might shift beneath her feet and fall out from beneath her like sand, dropping her back into the past, in a moment so close to this one it made her want to scream.

Colin, so angry over her refusal to sleep with him, revealing who he really was. What he really wanted from her.

If you don't want to put out, that's fine. But I have all those nice pictures of you. A very compelling video. Of what you did for me. I don't need sex. A little money from the media will be even nicer.

She'd thought she was smarter. More protected. Different.

She was the same foolish girl she'd always been. Worse, even, because this time the villain had succeeded in his seduction. He'd more than succeeded.

What she'd done with him…what she'd let him do to her…

"Alexios?"

The man in her bed stirred and Rachel tried not to pass out. Tried not to vomit. Or run screaming from the room.

She had to know what had happened. She had to know if he knew who she was.

Of course he does. Like he's here by accident? You can only be a naive fool to a certain point, moron.

"Alexios," she said his name again and he sat up, a wicked smile curving his face. When he actually looked at her, the smile faded.

As if he knew, even half asleep, that he wasn't waking to the postcoital scene he was hoping to be a part of. As if he knew that his response to the name had been wrong.

He'd probably already forgotten which woman he'd been in bed with. Which hotel.

That made her want to be violently ill. Or just violent.

But for the moment, she had to stay calm. She had to get answers.

"Rachel," he said, his voice as strong as whiskey and good sex, going straight to her head and making her toes curl. "You should come back to bed."

"I don't... No." She put her hand on her forehead. "Not right now. I..."

His eyes met with her hands. Where her fingers held his wallet. He looked back up at her, one black brow arched. Something in his manner changed. In an instant, he changed.

He pushed his dark curls off of his forehead and for a second she thought she was looking at a stranger. A naked stranger.

Then she realized that was what he was. She didn't know this man. Not at all. She'd fooled herself into thinking they'd shared something. That their souls had met, or some such idiocy. But they hadn't.

It only underlined her stupidity. Her weakness.

Last night, she'd felt like herself. Freed from all the layers of protection and expectation. Somehow slipped free of those well-meaning, soul-binding words spoken by her parents all those years ago. She'd felt real. Well, real Rachel was, it turned out, incredibly stupid. There was a reason she'd been kept in hiding.

"You know who I am, don't you?" she asked.

He stood, the covers falling from around his waist, his body, his beautiful hard body, on display for her. And even now it made her heart leap into her throat. Like it was trying to climb out so it could get a look at the view.

"Why were you looking at my wallet?"

"It was on the floor. I picked it up. I thought, 'nice wallet for a cabin boy.' Clearly far too nice. So now you might as well tell me the truth."

"I know who you are," he said. "Imagine my surprise when you found me before I could find you. Imagine my further surprise when I realized I didn't need a week or a special event to seduce you. You were a lot easier than I expected."

"To what end?" she asked, her heart thundering, her hands shaking. "Why would you... Why...?"

"Because I want what he has. Everything. And I've had something very special to him now. Now we both know I've had you first."

"You bastard," she said, scouring the room for her clothes. "You...! This is *my* hotel room." She stopped collecting her clothes and started getting his instead. "Get your clothes and get out." She threw his shorts at him, then his shirt. "Out!"

He started dressing. "I don't know who you think your fiancé is, but I know who he is."

"And I know who you are! A... A... I can't even think of a bad enough word for what you are. And you're no kind of man."

"You and I both know I am."

"The ability to trick a woman into letting you put your hard penis inside of her does not make you a man!"

"Did I trick you? Or did I, like you, not tell you everything. I hardly forced you into bed."

No, he hadn't. And that meant it was her fault. Her stupid, stupid fault.

"But you...seduced me knowing that you would ruin my engagement. With the express intent of doing it!"

"And you thought my seducing you would leave it intact? Is that it? Or are you just pissed because I planned it?"

"Yes! I am pissed that you planned it. I thought we had

something… I thought…" Her throat closed off, emotion, anger choking our her words.

"Such a virgin, Rachel," he said, his tone dry.

"No, I'm not, and I think we both know it. Because of you!" And even before that she'd lacked innocence. Which meant she should have known, she *did* know. But he'd made her forget.

"Because of you, *agape*," he said, tugging his slacks up and doing the button. "You made your choice. Don't be angry with me because I outed you as being faithless."

Before she could measure her response, his wallet was sailing out of her hands, skimming his ear, hitting the wall behind him. "Out!" she screamed.

She had just destroyed her engagement. The future of her family's company. All for sex. Sex with a man who'd been using her. Tricking her. Trying to hurt Ajax…

Ajax, who hadn't deserved this treatment at all. Who cared for her. And her father… After all he'd done for her…

She pressed her palms into her eyes, trying to keep the tears at bay. "Out. Out. Out," she said.

"Rachel…"

"You ruined my life!" she screamed, flinging her arms wide. "I thought you were different. I thought you made me…feel something and you were just lying. I blew up my life for you and it was a lie!"

"I never promised you anything. You made a mistake. Unhappily for you."

"Don't call him," she said, her stomach sinking. "Just don't call him."

"I don't have to," he said. "You won't marry him."

"One night with you and I'm going to leave the man I've been engaged to for years? I hardly think so," she said. Only a few moments ago, she would have. Just a few short moments ago.

She would have exposed herself to scandal, exposed her

family to it. She would have destroyed everything she'd spent years rebuilding for him. What had she been thinking?

And now…what had she done? What was wrong with her? She hadn't thought, not for a moment. She'd been feeling. Lost in some inane fantasy that had no hope of ever coming true.

Now she was sitting here, all of it burned down, ash at her feet, the hero of the story revealed as a villain.

"Just go. And please don't contact me. Please don't call him, don't… Don't."

"Now, why," he said, his lip curling, "would I agree to that? I got exactly what I wanted. I am a man who makes careful plans, *agape,* and I don't plan on changing them just because you shed a tear."

He strode across the room, to the hotel door, and walked out. He didn't even look at her again. Didn't spare her one more glance as he closed the door behind him.

Rachel sank onto the floor, her knees giving out entirely. And it was then she realized that she was still completely naked. But it didn't matter. Putting on clothes wouldn't make her feel less exposed. Wouldn't make her feel less… dirty.

That's what it was. She felt dirty.

She'd betrayed Ajax.

That was the truth no matter who Alex really was. But his betrayal was like salt in her wounds, as they would be salt in Ajax's.

Ajax…

She would have been prepared to end the relationship if there had even been a chance that…

That Alex wasn't a lying, horrible, hideous bastard. But there wasn't. He was. And that meant she had to go back home. The wedding had to go forward. Her life had to go forward. As if this hadn't happened.

This was why she'd avoided passion. This was why she'd avoided doing things that were risky, and crazy. Because when she took chances, she got hurt. Because when she trusted, it came back to haunt her. On her knees, her chest burning so bad she could hardly breathe, she remembered exactly why she'd taken to hiding herself.

Never again. She would go back to Ajax, to safety. And if Alex told him about tonight, she would beg for his forgiveness. She stared ahead, eyes dry and burning like her insides.

She would forget the heat and fire she'd discovered tonight. She would forget Alexios Christofides.

CHAPTER THREE

HE'D TOLD HIMSELF he wasn't going to the wedding. He'd told himself so as he'd boarded a plane in New York that was headed for Greece. He'd told himself so as he'd reclined in first class, accepting more glasses of wine than he normally would during travel.

He'd told himself so as he drove from the airport to the Holt Estate, where he knew the wedding was being held.

Everyone knew where the wedding was being held. It was international news. The wedding of enigmatic businessman and heartthrob Ajax Kouros to the beloved Holt Heiress. Photos of the event would cost a premium, the world waiting with bated breath for information, for a glimpse.

It had been shoved in his face on every news publication since he'd left Corfu. Since he'd been thrown out of Rachel Holt's bed.

Rachel.

He couldn't think of her without aching. That soft skin, that smile. The way she'd made love with him, all enthusiasm and clumsy motions. She had been inexperienced—well, non-experienced—but she had *wanted* him.

Never in his life had he been wanted like that. Not just in a sexual sense.

At some point over the course of that night he had forgotten. That he wasn't just Alex. That she wasn't just Rachel.

He had been a man, who wanted a woman. Not a man twisted and bent on revenge.

But her sweet voice piercing his sleep with *Alexios* had brought him straight back. And then it had all gone to hell. He hadn't enjoyed that moment. Hadn't enjoyed her realization that he was Ajax's enemy.

That fact had surprised him. And then when she'd asked, with tears in her eyes, that he not tell Ajax, he damn well hadn't done it.

And what was the point of going to all that trouble to have Ajax's woman if he didn't let him know it? He'd clearly passed the point of seducing her up the aisle so he could rob Ajax of his acquisition of Holt, a fact he'd learned was contingent on the marriage, so at the very least he could stop their marriage and deprive him of the company that way.

And yet he hadn't made the call.

It was a mystery to him. As was the fact that he was now at the Holt Estate with an expertly forged invitation. A forged invitation that allowed him to be one of the few guests admitted early to enjoy canapés and a tour of the grounds.

He'd had his personal assistant start working on the invitation a couple of weeks ago. Merely a precaution. And it had turned out to be a good thing, since he was here.

He hadn't been planning on coming, but it was always nice to cover your bases. If there was one thing Alex knew for sure, it was that life had no place for the lazy or the honest.

It was best to be hardworking and morally flexible.

He handed the invite over to the woman standing at a podium. She was dressed all in black, her blond hair pulled back into a neat bun. Everything about the décor, from the ribbons to the flowers, was restrained. Elegant. Nothing unnecessarily frilly or romantic.

The picture of the woman Rachel seemed to be in the

media, but not the woman he'd met that sun-drenched day in Greece.

He was filing that away. It could be useful information.

The woman scanned a code on the back of the invitation—that had been the tricky part, but his PA was friends with an acquaintance of Ajax's PA, which made getting in to reproduce the sequence on the codes possible—then smiled at him brightly when it made a nice sound that gave him the impression it had been approved, and gestured behind her.

"Follow the path to the garden. You'll find that refreshments are already being served, Mr. Kyriakis."

Nice alias. Seeing as he'd lived his entire adult life with one, he knew a good one when he heard it.

"Thank you."

He followed her instructions, and the neatly groomed path, to the back of the house. It was expansive, with rows of chairs set up facing an altar and the sea. Everything was white. Crisp and pure.

Again, very like the Rachel the media was so fond of. Nothing like the woman he'd experienced.

The woman he'd experienced hadn't seemed so pure when she'd been with him. Legs wrapped around his hips, her breath hot on his ear as she'd moaned her pleasure.

Heat washed over his skin. Prickles of sensation that bloomed from his neck and down his arms. He flexed his fingers, tried to shake off the sensation. It wasn't as though Rachel was the first woman he'd had.

There were any number of options available to a young man who found himself out on the streets and unsupervised from the age of fourteen. If nothing else, hooking up had often given him a bed to crash in, and he'd had no complaints about that.

So why on God's depraved earth was he so fascinated by a night of sex with a virgin? He couldn't fathom it.

Perhaps it was extra satisfying because he had taken her from Ajax. Because he'd robbed him of what he had been surely saving as a wedding night prize. Why else would he have left her untouched?

Just thinking about the man, being this close to him, made his stomach burn. If he hadn't decided years ago that assassination was a bad plan, he would have been considering it now.

Well, he was imagining it, but he wouldn't really do it.

He was a bastard—life had made him that way. But he wasn't entirely cold-blooded. Unlike Ajax.

Unlike their father.

No matter his position now, Ajax had been there, just as Alex had been. A young teenager who had taken advantage of the excess on offer.

The women, like Alex's mother, who would have done anything for their next fix. Who were slaves in every way. Victims. Living in poverty while surrounded by opulence. Kept on a leash of addiction, and in his mother's case, a strange attachment to the master of the manor.

A twisted thing she'd called love. The kind of love that, when severed, had left her to bleed out onto the floor. A crimson stain in Alex's memory that he could never wipe away.

Years and success wouldn't change that. Wouldn't bring her back. And yet Ajax stood at the top now, unaffected. With a family. A woman who had always appeared, to Alex, at least, to love him.

He looked unscathed, unspoiled. Ajax could pretend at respectability all he wanted but Alex knew the truth.

Because the truth was in him, too. But at least he never played as if he was anything other than a bastard. Ajax played as though he'd walked through it all and come out clean.

Alex *knew* he would never be clean.

He curled his fingers into fists and looked up at the house. There was a small group of people headed inside, led by a woman wearing black, which was clearly the uniform of the event staff.

He started in their direction, melting into the back of the group. Everyone was rapt, paying close attention to what the woman was saying about a fresco on the exterior wall that had been moved from an old church. Blah blah. He didn't care.

Greece was old. Like that was news.

He'd spent nights in more crumbling ruins than he could count. He was a fan of mod cons. As long as they didn't come at the price of living under the roof of a violent, sexually deviant psychopath.

Yeah, he'd preferred the ruins to that. He preferred the street to that. Starvation and cold and everything else that came with it.

He had run from that life. From all that it represented. He would not become a part of it.

He followed them into the house and as soon as they rounded the first corner, he separated from them and headed up the stairs. No one stopped him. Because he looked like he belonged. A right he'd earned, if only recently.

This was his world now. He was no longer someone who could be stepped on by the rich and powerful.

He *was* the rich and powerful. He went where he liked, he did what he liked.

"I have something to give the bride," he said to a passing servant. "Where might I find her?"

"Miss Rachel is in her suite. Down the hall and just to your left," the woman answered without blinking.

Because he looked the part. He spoke with confidence. And as a result, no one questioned whether or not he belonged.

He nodded once and continued on down where the woman had indicated.

He hadn't been going to come. But he was glad he had.

She'd never prayed so hard for her period to come in all her life. She'd never prayed for it to come. She'd taken it for granted. The cramps, the teariness. It had started when she was fifteen and it had gone on, regularly, for all the time since. Just a little signifier that it was the middle of the month. Nothing more.

Well, not right now.

Now the absence of it was about to send her into a panic attack. She'd been walking around her bedroom in her bra and panties for the past twenty minutes, a tampon on the nightstand, right next to an unopened pregnancy test.

Neither had been used at this point. One month since her night with Alex. One month of alternating between cursing his name and lying in a dark room just staring at the ceiling, unable to cry because tears were a release she wouldn't allow herself. A rush of emotion, too uncontrolled for the likes of her.

And then her period hadn't come. Even after it had passed fashionably late, she'd still been praying the floodgates might open and forth would come the crimson tide, and that the pregnancy test could remain unopened. But no such luck.

Tampon or test. She was going to be opening one of them in the next few minutes.

And it was rapidly becoming clear which.

She was already six days late. This little song and dance between her and those two items had been going on since the first morning.

She finally reached down and grabbed the pregnancy test.

And suddenly the world just sort of tipped to the side

and she saw herself clearly, standing there, almost ready to marry another man while she was potentially pregnant with Alex's baby.

And she knew there was no way she could get married today.

Her hands started shaking, her throat going dry. *Oh... Jax, please forgive me.*

So now she was just going to have to...tell him. Right before the wedding. But there was something she had to do first.

"Okay," she said to the little white-and-pink box. "Let's do this."

Her bedroom door swung open and she whirled around, clutching the box to her breasts in an instinctive attempt at modesty. Until she realized she was advertising that she was holding a pregnancy test and whipped it behind her back, her thigh crossing over the front of her other thigh in an attempt to hide that she was in very brief panties.

Then she froze, because she realized who her intruder was. For almost a full second, she was frozen, caught by those arresting blue eyes. Again.

It was almost like all that thinking about him had just... conjured him here. But at the worst possible moment.

His hair was shorter. His body wrapped in a custom-made suit and not in those thin, faded work clothes she'd first seen him in.

How strange to think it was the other Alex that had been a disguise, while this was the real him. It hardly seemed possible.

Then suddenly, she was hit by the bright, clear smack of reality. She hated Alex. *Hated* him. It was her wedding day. He was here. And she was afraid she was pregnant with his baby.

"What the ever-loving hell are you doing here?" she asked.

He seemed frozen. As she'd been only a moment before.

"At least close the door," she said, realizing that anyone who walked by was going to see her standing there in her undies.

He obeyed, stepping into the room.

"I am *naked*," she hissed.

"You're not."

"Close enough."

"Not anywhere near close enough." He was looking at her. Intently. As though he was trying to gauge the opaqueness of her underwear.

"Stop that! And what are you doing here?"

"I am here for your wedding, *agape.*"

"Weird. I don't think Ajax penciled his mortal enemy onto our guest list," she said, her fingers curling tightly around the pregnancy test still hidden behind her back.

She was trapped. Standing there in lacy bridal undies, unable to do anything for fear he'd see the test.

"He might have. Did you look to see if I was listed under Enemy or Mortal?"

"I was looking in the *A*'s for As—"

"I won't let you marry him," he said, his voice turning into a feral growl.

"What?"

"You don't know what he is."

She lifted one shoulder, the casual gesture at odds with her internal panic. With the fact that when he'd burst through that door he'd blown through her carefully cultivated, calm façade, yet again. "I've known the man for more than fifteen years. I think I know who he is."

"You've never even slept with him."

"I'm gonna," she said, edging away from him toward the bathroom, "tonight."

He strode toward her, blue eyes like chips of ice. He

put his arm around her waist and hauled her up against his chest. "You will not."

"Yes, I will," she said, words pouring out of her now, with no thought of control or decorum or any of the other stuff she was usually so attached to. She was lying, because before Alex had come in, she'd decided she couldn't do it. But she wanted to…hurt him if it was possible. To cause him some kind of discomfort because he sure had caused enough for her. "I'm going to have sex with him—" a shiver of displeasure coursed through her at the thought "—tonight. I'm going to let him inside of me. I'm going to do all the dirty naked things with him that I did with you!"

And then he leaned down and kissed her. As if he had every right to do it. As if she didn't have a wedding scheduled to happen in just four hours. As if she hadn't told him that she hated him and never wanted to see him again.

As if there was no reality. No Ajax. No vengeance gone wrong. No angry words. As if there was nothing more than passion. Fire and heat. She wrapped an arm around his neck, the other still behind her back, and parted her lips, let him slide his tongue against hers.

She kissed him back because for some reason, when Alex touched her, she couldn't think.

Because suddenly a month since the time they'd been apart didn't matter. And neither did anything else. Nothing but the kiss. The heat that flooded her body, her mind, her soul.

She wrapped her other arm around his neck and hit him in the ear with the edge of the box. He jerked his head back and looked to the side, and she followed his line of vision and froze.

Oh. Bloody perfect.

"What is this?" he asked, pulling back, his hand encircling her wrist.

"Nothing."

He arched a brow. "Try again."

"It is a…gift. For a friend."

"A gift for a friend?"

"Yessss," she said, drawing the word out to give herself time to think of more to add to her very stupid lie. "Because she asked for something that could tell the future and I thought…Magic 8 Ball or pregnancy test? And I went with pregnancy test because it gives specific yes or no answers to very specific questions."

"Do you think you're pregnant?"

"Right now? I think I'm absent a period. Which under normal circumstances would be like, 'Hey, great timing, because I'm supposed to be getting married.'"

"But?"

"Under the circumstances of 'I slept with my fiancé's enemy a month ago' I find it a bit worrisome, and yes, I think I might be pregnant."

"Go and find out," he said, moving away from her. "Now."

"So now I'm supposed to pee on your command? What if I don't have to go?"

"You were about to go—don't play that way."

His jaw was set, his skin pale. He wasn't taking this much better than she was. "Honestly, Alex, what do you care if I am?"

"I care because I will be a part of that child's life."

"You will not be," she said, the words coming out before she had a chance to think them through.

"You think I'm going to let that man near any child of mine?" he asked, rage rolling off him like a force field, pushing her back. "I know what happens to children who get near the Kouklakis family. I doubt you do."

"Ajax is…he's not a Kouklakis. He's…"

"Got an alias. How foolish are you? He's changed his name."

"I don't…"

"Go and take the test."

She didn't even have it in her to argue with him now. She nodded slowly, holding the box in numb fingers as she backed into the bathroom. Alex watched Rachel's retreating form, his heart pounding so hard he thought it might hammer through his chest and flop onto the bed, leaving a crimson stain on that pristine white duvet of hers.

A child.

His child.

This wasn't about revenge anymore. It hadn't been, not from the moment he'd claimed Rachel as his own. He wanted her, and he would have her. That was why he was here.

And because he refused to allow Ajax Kouros anywhere near a son or daughter of his.

No, Ajax didn't deal in human or drug trafficking, and Alex knew that. He knew, from the extensive research he'd done on the subject, that Ajax's business was entirely legitimate.

But bad blood was bad blood. Alex knew it. He felt it. He'd been born with the same blood as Alex, and he would never truly escape it. Alex hadn't, why should Ajax?

He shook it off. That thought. That burning sensation he felt whenever he imagined poison running through his own veins.

Things had changed for him.

Alex had made his fortune playing the stock market, first with other people's money, and now with his own. He was a gambler by nature, and doing it in the realm of the financial had been lucrative. Because like any good gambler, he had a skill for it. It wasn't pure luck, it was research. Memory. A natural feel for it.

It had earned him millions. On his twenty-sixth birthday, only six months ago, he'd netted his first billion.

He wasn't powerless anymore. He never would be again.

The bathroom door opened and Rachel appeared, white-faced, blue eyes watery.

"What?" he asked.

"There were two lines."

"Well, what does that mean?" he asked, tension making his heart race, pumping too much restless energy in his muscles.

"It means that I'm pregnant. And before you ask—it *is* your baby, I won't lie to you about that."

"You will not marry him."

"You know there are like…a thousand wedding guests coming? A hundred reporters?"

"You have two options, Rachel," he said, the adrenaline that was spiking through him making his mind run quickly. "You leave with me, now, don't speak to anyone. Or you go forward with the wedding. But mark my words, if you do that, I will stop the ceremony and I will tell everyone that you are pregnant with my child. That I seduced you in Corfu and that you gave it up to me in record time. Even without a paternity test, your precious Ajax will know. Because I'm the only man that's had you. And a due date with that big of a gap from your wedding night won't lie."

"The press…"

"The press is here, and they'll hear and report every word I say. But the decision is yours."

"It's not mine," she said, crossing her arms beneath her breasts. She was still wearing nothing more than her underwear. "I'm in an impossible situation here. I can't go back. I can't fix this. I can't…" she paused. "I could get a…" She looked away from him. "I could make it go away."

His stomach clenched. "No."

She shook her head, her blue eyes filling with tears. "You're right. I can't. I just… I can't."

"Come with me."

"And what?"

"Marry me."

CHAPTER FOUR

"YOU'RE INSANE," RACHEL SAID, aiming the air-conditioning vent at her face as Alex's red sports car peeled out of the driveway of the family estate.

Holy crap. She'd done it. She was running away from her wedding. She had…almost nothing. A few clothes, her favorite shoes. Her computer, her phone, her books.

But when he'd told her about the options, it was like seeing ahead, straight and clear. She could go out there, dressed all in white, the virginal bride, and promise herself to Ajax, knowing she was carrying another man's baby. Knowing the press would slaughter all involved if Alex strode down the aisle after her and told everyone in attendance what she'd done.

That was something she'd known she couldn't do even before she'd confirmed the pregnancy.

She knew the position she was in. She'd been made so fully aware of it that day in her father's office when he'd told her he would no longer shield her from the scandal she was exposing herself to.

She'd managed to stay perfect in the eyes of the public and because of that the media had placed her on a pedestal. That meant that any whiff of scandal would send a mob of reporters out to knock her straight off it.

Nobody liked a paragon, not really. They only kept her around for the chance to see her fall. She'd been spared that fate. Her father had protected her from the consequences of her actions, and after seeing the extent to which she could have ruined things for herself she'd decided that she would be playing the part of dutiful daughter, and wife, for the rest of her life.

And all she'd done was delay the inevitable—she saw that now.

It would be vicious when they found out about this, and no matter how she played this, she would come out the villain. She knew it for certain. But she didn't have the strength to have it happen in front of an audience. To let Alex say his piece like that, in front of all those guests and reporters, without any control for what was said or how.

The thought of it... It felt like her whole life, the life she'd taken such great pains to build from the time she was seventeen, was slipping through her fingers. She had become The Holt Heiress. Rachel Holt, style icon and media sweetheart. Eternal hostess, role model and...and what else she didn't know.

That night with Alex had brought something out in her she hadn't known had existed, and she was paying for it dearly now.

Stepping off that straight and narrow path had proven to have some pretty permanent consequences. And right now, she was taking a temporary leave of absence from those consequences. Because this way, she didn't have to look at Ajax's face when he found out. Or her father's.

Or Leah's.

She took her phone out. "I have to text Leah at least." She thought of her sister, who was all set to be maid of honor in the wedding. Her lovely, sweet sister who'd always gotten such crap from the press, but who was one of the best people Rachel had ever known.

It made her sick to think how Leah would worry.

How her father would worry.

And Ajax…

She had ruined everything. She was going to panic. She was officially on the verge of a panic attack.

"Don't text them until our plane is about to leave. And why am I insane?"

"Because *everything* is insane!" She exploded. "And you want me to marry you. I am not marrying you. I don't know you. I don't like you, either."

"How can you dislike me if you don't know me?"

"Fine. I don't know you very well, and what I do know about you, I don't like."

"You like my body."

"And if you were only a body, maybe that would matter. But there is, unfortunately, a personality beneath those hard muscles and it freaking blows."

"Does it?"

"You're a liar. You're hell-bent on ruining my fiancé's life, and I don't even know why, and you used me to get revenge on him."

"And then didn't do anything about it."

"You came today."

"Yeah, so I might have done something. But I wasn't going to come to the wedding so I wasn't planning on doing anything anymore. It's just…it's just that then I ended up coming. And it was a good thing I did."

"It was not."

"You would have married him then?"

"No."

"I thought not."

"Why do you hate him, incidentally? It seems like this might be really important to my future." She looked down at her hands and noticed they were shaking.

"As I told you, Ajax Kouros is a created name. A created identity. Hell, mine is, too, for the most part. Christofides is anyway. I was never called by a last name at all."

"How is that possible?"

"I was the son of a woman who couldn't remember her real name. Or if she did, she chose never to use it. 'Meli' was all she ever called herself. Honey. I think it was a double entendre of some kind. We lived in Ajax's father's compound. The infamous Nikola Kouklakis."

"What?"

"I suppose you've heard of him."

"The depth of that trafficking ring was...horrendous. When it was broken up a few years ago..."

"Yes, it was shocking. So many people. So many lives ruined. My mother wasn't one who was kidnapped. She was seduced. By the drugs. By the money. By love of some kind. We lived in the compound. As did Ajax. I remember seeing him and thinking he was quite something with his suits. The cars. But I learned very quickly to be afraid of him, because he was the big boss's son. Because what if he saw me causing trouble?"

"Alex...I don't... This can't be."

"What? You think I goad him for fun? I goad him because I don't think he deserves any of what he has, not while so many of us live with the lasting wounds of where his fortune came from."

"But he didn't earn any of it from...anywhere bad. He came to my family when he was a boy. He got work with my father. He built up from nothing."

"You don't know him like I do. You think you do, Rachel, but you don't know him."

"I do."

"Why had you never slept with him?"

"He's not...very passionate. And I figured I wasn't, either, so fine."

He chuckled, a dark, humorless sound. "I witnessed some of his behavior back at the compound. He was with the women there. He's certainly not passionless, and knowing his background I find it worrisome more than anything that he hasn't touched you. Perhaps he was just going to savor your virginity."

Her face heated, anger and anxiety shooting through her. "He didn't know I was a virgin. I had a…a relationship before him, and I didn't… I obviously didn't sleep with him, but it wasn't chaste. Okay? And Ajax and I never discussed it, so he really didn't know."

"Trust me, *agape,* he knew."

"*You* didn't."

"I only knew you for an afternoon."

"It had some lasting consequences," she said, leaning against the window of the car and watching the scenery fly by. "Why am I going with you again?"

"You don't want me destroying your reputation in the press? Or destroying Ajax at the altar, though I can't imagine why."

Her head was swimming. She couldn't even imagine the Ajax she knew, the man who seemed to spend twenty-four hours a day in a crisply pressed suit, prowling the halls of a drug house and mingling with prostitutes. It didn't make sense.

"I only know what I know about him."

And that of all the things that she felt right now—which were blessedly cushioned by shock or she would be rocking in a corner— heartbreak wasn't one of them. So the other thing she could add to the list of Very Obvious Things She Knew was that she did not love Ajax, for certain.

That part of her was relieved to be fleeing the wedding, even if it was with Alexios Christofides.

Even if she was having his baby.

Her stomach pitched. No, she wasn't relieved about that. She couldn't even really think about all that.

"You aren't going to hold me prisoner, are you?" she asked when the car pulled up to the airport.

"If I wanted to do that, I would have done it back in Corfu."

"I suppose."

"There's no *suppose* about it. I had you wrapped around my finger, *agape mou.*"

She gritted her teeth and opened the door to the car. He followed, and an employee came out for their bags. Not the normal treatment, even when *she* flew, and she was accustomed to first class.

She whirled around to face him. "Actually, Alex, no matter what you say, no matter what your plan was, I'm fairly confident I had you wrapped around mine."

"You had me by something, but it wasn't my finger."

She curled her lip. "You're despicable. Now which terminal are we going to?"

"We are taking a private plane. All the better for us to discuss our issues."

"Why do I feel like I'm in the presence of the big bad wolf?"

"Because of my big…teeth?"

She made a face. "Maybe it's your ego, did you ever think of that?"

"It could be that," he said, obviously completely unbothered by her insults.

"I don't like you," she said. For some reason, with him, the honesty flowed.

"I know, but you still want me, and that really bothers you."

Her hackles rose, because, dammit, it was true. "Not half as much as having your baby bothers me."

"Then why are you coming with me?"

She shook her head and stopped walking. "Because… because as angry as I am at you, this isn't all your fault. Not really. I blew up my future. I put a bomb in the middle of it and now it's so wrecked there's no putting it back together. If I stay, I expose my family to more scandal than if I go quietly."

"And how it affects your family is what really matters to you?"

"It matters. My mother was the most lovely, gracious woman around. No one ever found fault with her. My father is so…decent and my sister gets hell from the press for no reason other than they wanted a punching bag and they picked her. I can't make things worse for them."

"What about you?"

"Fine. Me, too. I don't want cameras in my face, and lots of questions asked. And…Alex, you're the father of this baby, whether I like you or not. And I feel like you deserve a chance. Not marriage, mind you, but a chance."

"So what is it you want?" he asked.

"To know you, would be a good start."

"I take it you don't mean in the biblical sense."

"I already do, and it got me nowhere but pregnant and out of a wedding, so let's just hope that the other kind of getting to know you goes better."

"If you expect me to sit around and talk about my feelings, you're out of luck. If, however you would like to get to know me more closely in the biblical sense…"

"I'm thinking of two words here, Alex, and they are brought to you by the letters *F* and *U*."

"I had the impression you were a docile little thing, based on media reports. And also that you weren't very smart."

Heat streaked across her cheekbones. "I suppose you did, but then that's the way the media likes to show me, I guess." Partly by her design. "Simple and accommodating."

"And you aren't."

"Not on the inside," she muttered.

But she'd learned to be. After all the parties had started catching up with her. After Colin and his sleazy seduction that had concluded with her agreeing to some drunken, pornographic photos and a brief video.

One she'd had to confess the existence of to her father. If there was anything more horrifying on the face of the planet she couldn't think of it. Hard evidence of just how stupid she was being. And as her father had pointed out, she was lucky that the worst of it was the photos. Going off alone, drunk with a man who was essentially a stranger could have ended much worse.

Then there had been the partying, the drugs she'd been experimenting with. The fact that she'd been driving herself home under the influence...

She'd deserved the dressing down her father had given her. The threats of being cut off. And as she'd looked at the pictures of herself with Colin...it had been a full-color exhibit of her bad choices.

The wake-up call she'd badly needed. And after the photos and video had been managed, after Colin had been paid off, her mother had gotten sick. Rachel had thrown herself into caring for her mother, driving her to appointments, keeping her company, helping her plan her parties. Helping host them.

And then on the other side of that, after her mother's death, had been Ajax.

Her father had expected her to marry him. Of course, her father also hoped she would love Ajax. Either way, she'd known what she was supposed to do.

Ajax treated her like she was fine china he was afraid to break. Unlike Alex, who seemed to think she could withstand all manner of rough treatment. Brute.

She sniffed. Loudly.

"What?" he asked.

"You aren't very nice to me," she said, walking ahead of him, following the cart that held their luggage. "Interesting you claim Ajax is such a villain but he treated me like a—"

"Nun."

"—a princess."

"You aren't a damn princess. You're just a regular woman."

"Ajax thinks I'm a princess."

"In about four hours Ajax will think of you as that traitor who left him at the altar."

She clenched her teeth together tightly. She couldn't argue with that. And she couldn't blame all of this on him, not when she absolutely had a stake in the guilt. But she really, really wanted to.

The conversation stopped when they approached a sleek jet parked on the runway. The door opened—a carpeted staircase waited to ease their entrance.

"Swank," she said, going up the stairs and into the plane, where her tart descriptor was proven to be an understatement.

Everything was beautiful beyond belief, polished and plush, from the cream-colored floor to the soft leather couches.

"There's champagne chilling," Alex said, coming in behind her. "Of course, you can't have any. Bad for the baby."

"Are you always this insufferable?"

"Are you?"

"No, I never am. I'm actually extremely pleasant, all the time. It's just that you make me… There really isn't a word strong enough to express the anger-slash-anxiety I feel when you're around."

"Attraction?"

She narrowed her eyes. "That's not the word."

"You're sure?"

"I am *so* sure."

"Then why did you kiss me earlier?"

She sat down on the couch, suddenly feeling taxed. "You also make me crazy. I do stupid things when you're around."

"I'll take that as a compliment."

She crossed her arms. "I wouldn't. Can you at least get me an orange juice?"

"That, I could manage." He pushed a button on his arm rest and gave the order.

She leaned back and crossed her arms. "Where are we going, anyway?"

"Back to my house. Away from the media firestorm that will no doubt ensue when they realize the bride has failed to show up for the wedding of the century. You'll have to face the fallout eventually, but why not put it off for a while?"

It really did sound good. To avoid reality for just a bit.

"You can text your sister now."

Oh, yes, that was a bit of reality she really couldn't avoid. Otherwise her family would be sending the police after them. For a couple of seconds she entertained the idea of letting them arrest Alex for kidnapping. But that was a news story she didn't really want her child going back and reading, so she decided against it.

Rachel pulled out her phone, her fingers hovering above the letters on the screen. What did you say when you did something like this?

"Why aren't you texting Ajax, by the way?"

"Because I'd rather roll around in honey and get thrown into a badger den."

Short and sweet, Rach. Don't tell all yet. She looked across at Alex, who was now sprawled in the armchair like a lazy big cat. Twitching his tail, waiting for his prey to make a false move.

Yes, the less she said about the situation, the better. She knew next to nothing about it except that she couldn't marry Ajax. And that she had to figure out what she was going to do about Alex.

I'm not coming. I need to be with Alex. I'm sorry. Please tell Jax that I'm sorry.

She took a deep breath, then hit Send on the exhale.

"Done. I told them."

"What exactly?"

"That I'm not coming. Nothing more. Well, I mentioned you. Your first name."

"We'll see how long it takes Ajax to send a hit man."

"Actually," she said, as the plane engine started and they began to taxi around the runway, "I'm curious."

"About?"

"Why didn't you stop the wedding? Why didn't you call Ajax and gloat? Why weren't you hanging your sheet stained with my virgin's blood out your window like some kind of marauding knight or whatever?"

He cleared his throat. "You kicked me out—I didn't have time to take the sheet."

"And that foiled your evil plan?" He said nothing in response. "I'm serious," she said.

"Did it occur to you that maybe things changed because you were the one who found me?" he asked.

The stewardess came in with a tray of drinks. What looked like a scotch for Alex, the jerk, and an orange juice for her. She thanked the woman and wrapped her fingers around the glass, letting the coldness seep into her skin.

"I… No," she said. "I hadn't really thought of it. But… it is true. I am the one who found you."

"Strange, don't you think?"

"Maybe." More than strange. But there was no denying it. There was no way to accuse him of putting himself in her path, either. She'd seen him first. She'd approached him. And unless his ego was even bigger than she imagined, he'd had no way of knowing she would have to go and talk to him when she saw him. That she would be hit with a bolt of attraction so intense it left her stunned and utterly senseless.

"I was there for you," he said slowly, swirling the contents of his glass before taking a sip. "I won't lie about that. I was there to find you and seduce you. But I had a plan, you see. You had a fundraiser later in the week."

"I ended up not going." She looked down into her juice.

"I know," he said.

"How?"

"Because I went."

"Oh." She cleared her throat. "Why?"

"I don't know," he bit out. "But I was going to meet you there, at that fundraiser. And seduce you with my wealth and fortune. Seduce you away from my rival, slowly. Publicly. I was going to bring you over to my side of things and make him watch powerlessly as I did so."

"And then what was supposed to happen to me?"

He shrugged. "That was of no concern to me. But instead, you found me on a dock after I'd just come in to Corfu. What are the odds of that?"

"Heck if I know," she said.

"I wouldn't know, either."

"So what... So that's why you didn't tell Ajax? That's why you didn't call weeks ago and have the wedding called off?"

"I was as seduced as you were," he said. "Though I hate to admit it. If I'd had any respect for my own plan I would have followed it. Instead..."

"Instead we met and spent the day together and then we..."

"Spent the night together."

"And then it all went to hell," she said.

"When I came to your house today... What I came for... It had nothing to do with revenge. I was there for you."

Their eyes locked, electricity crackling between them, her heart pounding so hard she thought she might pass out.

Her phone buzzed and she looked down. She had a message from Leah.

Alex who? Anyone I know?

Well, what was the point in lying? It was going to come out. The press would see her with Alex. She would have to explain eventually that she was pregnant. And who the father was.

She might as well let the bomb drop in stages. She typed in a reply.

You don't know him. Alex Christofides. Unexpected. And I'm sorry.

It was sort of a lie. Leah wouldn't know him. But Ajax would. And the way she'd phrased it made it sound like she didn't know who he was. Also a lie.

She was big into self-protection at the moment.

Well, who wasn't? Except for Alex. That was a strange thought, but when she looked back at their night together…

When she'd confronted him, he'd been honest. About why he'd seduced her. About who he was. It didn't make a lot of sense, really.

"Why didn't you defend yourself?" she asked. "Why didn't you lie?"

"Because I couldn't think," he said.

It pained Alex to admit it, but it was the truth. He hadn't been able to think up a lie with her looking at him as though he'd personally stabbed her in the chest. Because somehow, during the course of their day together, his seduction had been genuine.

He had wanted her. It had been easy to forget just who

she was. Who she belonged to. He didn't look at her and see Ajax Kouros's fiancée.

He'd looked and seen Rachel. So soft and elegant, with wildness that ran strong beneath.

He'd seen her. And he had wanted her with every piece of himself.

So he'd taken her, and when she'd confronted him, he'd been able to do nothing but speak the truth because he'd deviated so far from his plan he had no idea how to get back to it. He should have lied. Appealed to her. Kept to the original plan.

But he hadn't, and it was too late to go back now.

He would have let her go if it was what she'd wanted. But things were different now. She was pregnant and that meant he had to keep her.

He ignored the slug to the gut that rebelled at the idea of allowing her to marry Ajax, pregnant or not. Of course, had she wanted to do so, he wouldn't have stopped it. He could have let her go.

The inability to do so would imply that she was special. That he had feelings for her.

Alex didn't have time for feelings.

He'd made time in his life for two things: making money and getting revenge. Everything else was an incidental. A distraction he couldn't afford.

Of course, now that there would be a child he'd have to make room for a third thing.

Because he would be damned if any child of his left to be raised by a stranger. If any child of his wasn't in his sight at all times.

Alex knew about all the evil in the world, and if there was any way for him to shield his own child from it, he would do so.

As though his own life depended on it.

CHAPTER FIVE

HIS ISLAND WAS BEAUTIFUL. He would never get tired of it. Of the fact that it was his. Of the fact that he now owned a place he possessed total control over.

Back in the compound, everything had been shared. Perhaps *share* was too generous a word. It had been fought over. There had been a serf class in the compound. The women, the security guards. And the security guards had had guns, which put the women square on the bottom rung.

And beneath that...

The children of those women.

Many of them had been given away by their mothers. Sold, Alex now realized, for drugs. He had spent many years feeling astonished, grateful, that his mother hadn't done so. That she'd put some sort of value on him. That he'd stayed safe.

A miracle, it had seemed.

But then he'd found out the truth. And the truth hadn't been rainbows and a mother's love. No. The truth had been poison.

He was the monster he'd always despised. A tool that kept his mother near her favorite addiction. Not heroin, but Nikola Kouklakis himself.

The older man had, of course, kept her there since she was the mother of his son. Since *Alex* was his son. But Alex had discovered the truth and when his mother was no longer useful it had all come crashing down.

And Alex had run. Run away and never looked back.

And when he'd finally stopped, when he'd won enough card games that he had some money—money and this island—met enough people that he'd forged business connections and learned about the stock market, when he'd finally reached the pinnacle of success, that was when he'd looked back for the first time.

He'd looked back at all of the pain, all of the injustice, and then he'd looked at the one man who had risen above it. Clean, pristine and well-respected. Rich as god with a beautiful woman hanging on his arm.

And he'd known that next on his agenda was making sure that Ajax Kouros knew helplessness. That he knew fear. That he knew what it was to lose the things he loved.

And while he hadn't destroyed the other man's business yet, not for lack of trying, he did have Ajax's fiancée.

And though he wasn't actively using Rachel as revenge at the moment, that thought almost made him cheerful.

"Where are we?" Rachel asked as the plane touched down, white sand and turquoise sea rushing into view.

"An island near Turkey. I call it…" And he realized that earlier he'd told her his mother's name. It made him feel exposed, to tell her what he called the island when she would know why. He cursed his moment of sentimentality. Cursed the fact that he still cared so much for a woman who'd never loved him back. Who had ended her life rather than spend her days with him. "I call it Meli's Hideaway," he said. "And before you ask, no, my mother never saw it. She…died just before I left the Kouklakis compound. But if she hadn't…this is where I would have taken her. So she could have a rest, finally. Though she's resting now, I suppose." If she had given him a chance. If she had trusted in him at all. If the idea of being with him hadn't been a torture she couldn't bear.

"I'm sorry," she said, her voice muted. "My mother passed away, too. It's hard. Really hard."

"Life is hard,' he said, lifting one shoulder in a casual gesture.

"What? That's it?"

"I'm sorry," he said. "Life is hard and then you die. Is that better?"

She shook her head. "Not really. You're not exactly enjoying the journey, are you?"

He stood up as the plane came to a stop. "Enjoying the journey is for another sort of person, from another sort of life. Someone like you, *agape*."

"Well, I won't deny that I have a great family. That I've been blessed to have a lot of nice things. Yes, I do enjoy the journey." She was lying, though. He could sense it. Strange because when he'd met her in Corfu, she had exuded light. Joy. But he didn't see those things in press photos of her.

It was like she was hiding that light most of the time.

"Were you going to enjoy spending the rest of your journey with Ajax?"

She nodded, her posture stiff. "Of course I would have. I care about him deeply."

"But you don't love him."

"Oh, bah. Why are you people so fixated on love?" Alana had tried to talk her out of the wedding at the eleventh hour. Citing love as the primary reason. "I like him. I love him in a way. Sure it's not an all-consuming kind of love, but—"

"But you aren't crying your eyes out just at this moment, either," he said.

"I have a lot on my plate here," she said. "I just found out I'm pregnant." She paused and swore. "Pregnant. Oh…I can't *even*. I can't even take all of this in. And I just ran out on my wedding. And I'm in Turkey. With you."

"We're not in Turkey. We're on my island."

"Yeah, big effing difference to me just at the moment."

"If it's any consolation, I feel similarly…run over. Is that how you feel?"

"Run over by a train, yes."

"This doesn't have to be difficult," he said. He was about to propose marriage again. Yes, she'd brushed his mention of marriage off the first time, but she'd been shocked. She would come around, he was certain of it.

One thing he knew for sure, and that was that he refused to be a shadowy figure in the background of his child's life. He would not be that man. He would be as different from his own father as humanly possible. As different from everyone in his family as humanly possible.

If you can be.

No. He wasn't the same. He would love his child. He wouldn't want to own his child, wouldn't keep that child around simply to keep a link between himself and the person he was…obsessed with.

He would never be either of his parents.

"How is it going to be easy?" she asked as the door to the plane opened and a rush of thick, warm air filled the cabin.

"Perhaps it will fall somewhere between easy and difficult?"

"Perhaps," she said, walking toward the exit.

"You don't sound convinced."

"I'm not." She descended the stairs and he followed, his eyes on her curves, the way her white capris cupped her expertly. He was still a man, after all, regardless of how intense the day had been.

And she was still a temptation. It had nothing to do with how provocative her clothing was. It wasn't, in truth. She exuded class. A kind of untouchable, crisp elegance that a man like him had rarely been exposed to.

Rachel Holt had come by her style and poise due to a lifetime of being immersed in wealth and culture, of being aware of cameras watching her every move.

Nothing like the way he'd grown up.

It was part of what he found so enticing. That prim little exoskeleton of hers. Perfect hair and makeup, even just after finding out she was pregnant and running out on her wedding. But he'd cracked all that open. Had seen her skin flushed pinker than that top she was wearing. Had seen her hair in disarray, her skin glistening with sweat…

He'd had those expertly polished nails dug deep into his shoulders, and that was something he couldn't forget.

He shifted and tried to ease the pressure caused by his growing arousal. Nothing helped. Not when he had the back of Rachel Holt as his view. The rest of the island just didn't seem to matter. And neither did anything else.

"And why is that?" he asked.

"Because I…don't think I like you." She looked up and around at the cypress trees that spread around them to create a canopy of green, and at the white sand beaches beyond them.

"There are some incredible ruins on this island. Colonial and Ottoman."

"I was just in Greece. Ruins, we have them."

"I am aware," he said. "I was trying to make conversation."

"Do you live in a ruin? Or do you have an actual house?"

"I have a house, but some people would argue I live in ruin."

She snorted. "At this point, some people would argue that I do, too."

"You are giving off a bit of a fallen-woman vibe," he said dryly.

"Am I?" She sniffed her wrist. "I don't feel any different."

He turned and looked at her. "Not at all?"

Her cheeks flushed a deep rose. "No."

"Interesting. Would you like to walk to the house or drive?"

"You're in a tux," she said. "You're hardly dressed to walk."

He looked down. "Indeed not. I'm a little disoriented. Could be because in New York it's early morning. Which means I've technically been up all night."

"You came from New York?"

"Yes."

"Why?"

He looked at her, at those cheeks, still flushed from the sun and from…from whatever memories had come into her mind when he'd looked at her. "I came for you."

"That simple?"

"Yes."

"Why did you come for me?"

"I don't know," he said, and it was the honest truth. "Because I don't want him to have you. Because I want you for myself. Because I think you're beautiful and as of now you're the only woman I can imagine having in my bed, and considering I would like to have sex sometime soon that's very inconvenient, and even more so if you were to marry another man."

She blinked. "That's almost flattering."

"Almost. A walk, I should think." He took his jacket off and cast it onto the sand, then rolled his shirt sleeves up. "It might do something to shake off the time change."

"Lead the way then."

He started down a path that took them down near the beach and could have sworn at the absurdity of getting sand in his custom-made shoes. Shoes he'd bought with his own money and not the money earned by other people's suffering. There, a reminder that he had transcended his blood in some way.

"So what do you do in New York?" she asked.

"I gamble with other people's money."

"What?"

"I deal in investments," he said. "And I'm very good at it."

"Isn't that a bit unstable?"

"Sure. Can be. But I've made enough of a profit that I'm sitting on stable assets of my own, and I've made some wise purchases and investments myself."

"Including an island."

"I won this," he said.

"You won it?"

"In a card game. It was one of the more interesting gambling experiences of my life. Yes, I was a literal gambler there for a while. At first with other people's money."

"How?"

"Card counting is a particularly useful skill. I happen to have the gift. I was a kid living on the streets doing card tricks for tourists and a rich guy picked me up, offered to kit me out to play in the casinos with his money, for a cut. I said 'of course,' naturally."

"Naturally," she said.

"I won a lot of money. And I got to keep part of it. Rented myself an apartment, started offering up an underground service. Until I had enough money to go gamble for myself at least once a week."

"And?"

"I ended up in a high rollers' game. There were things in that pot by the end that you wouldn't believe, including a night with a man's wife, which I turned down, by the way. But the island... I took the island."

She looked hard at him, blue eyes glittering. "You're really twenty-six, Alex?"

"Yes. And I was eighteen when I was doing that. From there, I figured I better decide what to do with the money I'd earned. So I walked away from the casino and started looking into investing. And I proved to have a knack for that so I thought…why not do it for other people? An extension of where I came from."

"A self-made man," she said.

He laughed. "None of us are really self-made, Rachel. We're made with the aid or misfortune of other people. In my case, people had to lose money so I could gain it. Now, the people I make money for are aided by me, as I am by them. You are made by your father, by the media, and you were to be finished by Ajax, am I right?"

"Finished?"

"It's how you were going to spend the rest of your life in comfort. You found a man who would close the loop neatly on everything you've built."

"I don't think of it that way."

"No?"

"No." She wobbled in the sand and he reached over and caught her arm, holding her steady. She froze for a moment, her eyes falling to his lips. She swallowed hard. "I don't think of it…of him…that way. It's not how it is."

"Then how is it?"

"I don't know. He's a friend. And…maybe like a brother, almost, which I can see right at this moment is so ridiculous it's… I don't know why I thought I could marry him. I don't know why at all. I thought caring could be enough. I thought it was enough."

"Only because you'd never had passion." He'd been the one to show that to her.

"Don't be so smug—it's nasty. Truly, I wouldn't crow about it if I were you. Is there an easier conquest than a woman who's still a virgin at my age? 'Hard up' doesn't even begin to describe it."

"That's not what it was though. I myself was not particularly hard up, as you call it, and I still felt the electricity between us."

She stopped short, arched one eyebrow. "Oh, really?"

"Yes," he said. "Don't deny that you felt it."

"No, I mean, 'oh, really, you weren't hard up?' What does that mean? When was the last time you were with someone else?"

"Jealousy, Rachel? I didn't think you liked me."

"I'm not jealous. I'm curious."

"And if I tell you, you won't be angry?"

"I've been angry at you for a solid month, Alexios. I'm not making you any guarantees on that score. You could breathe funny and make me angry at this point."

"Don't be dramatic. It had been a couple weeks by the time I met you."

She sniffed loudly as she'd done at the airport, a sign of her pique, he was realizing. "It had been twenty-eight years when I met you, but whatever."

"Are you saying I'm special, Rachel?"

"Heck. No. I am not saying that. I am not saying that even a little bit. I'm just saying—some of us don't run around with our pants around our ankles all the time."

"And you're sure that Ajax was celibate the whole time you were together?"

"I…I just… I… Yes."

"Probably you're delusional," he said. "As you were about marrying him in the first place."

"Okay, Alex, answer this question. Has there been a woman since you were with me?"

"No." She looked far too triumphant when he admitted that. This honesty thing where she was concerned really had to stop.

She seemed to bring it out in him. He'd held back next to nothing since he'd met her. He'd told her. About why he'd seduced her, about his mother, about why he hated Ajax.

Well, he'd told her most of it. There were things he couldn't bring himself to speak out loud into an empty room. Much less share with with anyone else.

His house came into view. He'd had it custom built when the island passed into his control. It was completely modern. Square, with hard, clean edges, windows that faced the sea. There was no gilded excess, no old-world opulence.

That would have reminded him too much of the Kouklakis compound. And he had no interest in that. It was too much in his mind as it was.

Stale, filthy opulence. And a carpet stained with blood.

"It's certainly different," she said.

"Is it?"

"Very…minimalist."

"I'd had enough Persian rugs and intricate carvings to last a lifetime. I wasn't interested in living in it for the rest of my life."

"Oh."

"What about you?" he asked. "What sort of architecture do you prefer?"

Rachel paused on the path, his question hitting a nerve for some reason she couldn't really identify. "I don't know."

"You don't know what sort of house you would have liked to live in one day?"

"Ajax's house," she said, bristling. "And his penthouse in the city. All nice places. And nothing not to like about them."

"And before that?"

"I had an apartment. In New York." She'd liked her apartment a lot, but she'd given it up before the wedding, naturally. But it hadn't been a place for entertaining. It had been a place just for her. Giving it up had been a lot harder than she'd anticipated, in truth, but it wasn't worth crying over. "And when I come to Greece I stay in the family vacation house."

"If you were going to have a home built, what would it be like?"

"I don't know, okay? I've never thought about it, but what does it matter? I was going to have a beautiful home with Ajax. Now I may very well end up being homeless because I just walked away from a deal that was essential to both my father and to Ajax. Because… Because…"

Suddenly her fists tightened. "You knew," she said, her tone getting cold. "You knew and you're over here pretending to be all honest and 'marry me' and crap, but you knew."

He didn't blink, his blue eyes focused on her.

"Whoever marries first gets my father's company. That's what you want. It's not me, or hurting Ajax by taking my virginity or whatever else. It's that you were going to try and get me to marry you so that you could screw him out of Holt. You're trying to take my family business!"

"Rachel…"

"You—"

"If I had wanted that, if that was the route I'd decided to take, I would have sweet-talked you back in Corfu when you saw my ID. As it is, I let you go."

"And then you came back. Were you going to make some sort of declaration of love and try to woo me away from the wedding and to…Vegas or something?"

The thing that was so unsettling about that prospect was the fact that it might have worked. That if she hadn't found out she was pregnant, if he'd walked in and kissed her, and told her that he hadn't stopped thinking about her for the past month, that he loved her, she would have probably dropped everything and run away with him.

Because she had feelings for him. Feelings that she

couldn't quite understand or deal with, but they were definitely feelings. Stupid, *stupid* feelings.

Feelings that should be utterly choked out by this most recent revelation.

"I don't understand. Even if the past that you share—that you say you share… Even if it's true I don't know why you would want to destroy him so badly."

"Of course you don't," he said, walking in front of her, toward the house, "because you live in a dream world, little girl. You don't know anything about the way the world works. And you should be thankful for that."

CHAPTER SIX

RACHEL LAY DOWN on the white down-filled blanket and stared at the ceiling. She would ask for him to take her home if she wasn't such a coward. If she wasn't so afraid she didn't have a home to go back to.

Even if she did, it would be crawling with reporters, ready to get the juicy dirt on why she'd left Ajax at the altar. And the lame thing was there was tons of juicy dirt. If the bride being pregnant with another man's baby wasn't a great scandalous headline, she really didn't know what was.

Society wedding of the century became farce just that quickly and the press would absolutely adore it.

There was a knock on the door. Not Alex, (A) because he wouldn't have knocked, and (B) because it was soft, a woman's hand, she was almost certain.

"Yes?"

The door opened a small woman with dark hair came in. "Mr. Alex has requested that you join him for dinner out on the terrace."

"Oh, has he now?"

"Yes," the woman said, either not picking up on Rachel's annoyance, or choosing not to acknowledge it.

"When does he expect me?"

"Ten minutes, miss."

"Tell him it will be twenty—I need to dress for it. And tell him not to let that go to his head."

The woman nodded and backed out of the room. Rachel felt like a shrew. A sweaty, mean one. She was hot from the walk, still, and in a foul mood.

A quick shower did wonders for the sweaty part, but the meanness still seemed to be simmering beneath the surface, even while she slipped into a simple black shift dress and a pair of black heels. She fastened a string of pearls around her neck and looked at her side profile. Her hair was neat, in place as it should be. Her makeup looked good.

She looked normal. Like the Rachel she was accustomed to seeing in the mirror every day.

Which was so strange because she didn't feel like normal Rachel. She hadn't. Not since that day she'd locked eyes with stupid Alexios Christofides.

She let out a harsh breath and exited her room to find the maid standing there waiting for her.

"I will take you to Mr. Alex."

"Thank you," Rachel said, even while she thought that he was only sending her an escort to make sure she didn't bribe his pilot to get her off the island.

That was when she realized how stuck she was. With each step across the white marble floor and out toward the terrace, she felt a rope tightening around her neck, her pearls suddenly feeling heavy, like they were choking her.

She reached up and unfastened them as they walked, wadding them up in her shaking hand, holding them down at her side.

"Miss Rachel," the maid said, announcing her as though she were a duchess of some kind.

Alex stood and her heart squeezed. No matter how angry she was, he never failed to leave her utterly speechless. He was wearing a simple white button-up shirt, unfastened at the collar, the sleeves rolled up past his forearms.

His skin looked a deeper bronze in that color, a glimpse

of chest hair visible through the open neck. He looked so effortless. So ridiculously sexy.

It wasn't fair.

It wasn't fair that her body was drawn to a man like this. A man who had tricked her, used her and basically had her held captive on an island. What the ever-loving heck was wrong with her? Was she punishing herself for past sins? Or was there something that drew her to men who wanted to…use her?

She sat down, and he took his seat.

"I trust you had a nice rest?" he asked.

"I don't think you really trust that. I'm sure you know I spent the past hour quietly freaking out in the privacy of my bedroom."

"I suppose that's only fair."

"I've just found out I'm having a baby, on top of everything else, so yes, it is only fair."

"That is why I proposed marriage," he said. "Not to get Holt away from Ajax, but for the sake of the baby."

"Great. Fine. But please know that I will not marry you. Not for the baby, not for anything. At the very least not until my sister is married and I am certain, one hundred percent certain, that you won't get Holt because of my indiscretion. I will not allow you to hurt Ajax or my family in that way." A startling thought occurred to her. "And if you go after my sister I will be forced to remove your male member from your body with a very dull pocketknife, and don't think I won't do it. I might have been spoiled from birth, but I'm also from New York, and we don't mess around over there."

"I have no desire to go and seduce your sister," he said, leaning back in his chair, looking out at the ocean. As though they were discussing the weather, and not her desire to castrate him. "My plans, my priorities, have changed. My loyalty is to the child, not to my vengeance."

"Well, it's very early in the pregnancy, and things can go wrong, so, yet again, marriage is off the table."

"Fine. For you, maybe it is, but not for me. I'll continue to enter it into the discussion at times I feel are appropriate."

"You are a massive pain in the rear, do you know that?"

"I absolutely do," he said, lifting a glass of wine to his lips. Yeah, and he was drinking wine in front of her. He knew he was a pain. And he seemed to revel in it.

"Well, stop it." She took a sip of water from her glass.

"Probably not. That's twenty-six years of bad habits you're asking me to break immediately, and I doubt it's going to happen."

"Another good reason to avoid marrying you."

"Why is it you agreed to come with me?"

"I'm a massive coward," she said. "Among other things."

"What other things?"

"An idiot. That's the other thing I am. I can't believe I fell for your charm and that boyish curly thing your hair does when it's wet and your...sparkling blue eyes."

"Are you preparing to compose a sonnet about me?"

"Shall I compare you to a horse's ass?"

"Is that your attempt at poetry?"

"Yes. I thought it was good."

"Brilliant." He took another sip of wine.

"I have to ask, Alex, because it doesn't make a lot of sense to me—what does a guy like you want with a baby?"

"I don't want *a* baby," he said. "I want *my* baby and that's an entirely different thing."

"Just a bit-of-sperm different at this point. It's not like you know the child, not like you could even...feel him or get an idea he was inside of me for...months and months. I would think walking away from it would be really easy for you."

"Why is that?"

She lifted a shoulder. "Because a lot of men do. It's not

an insult, it's just that…well, a lot of men do. And since you just picked me up with the idea of getting revenge on Ajax and that's all done, I would have thought it wouldn't serve your purpose to be involved with the child. Especially since I won't marry you and let you take Holt from Ajax."

"This is a matter of honor."

"You have honor? Where was your honor when you were stealing my virtue in Corfu?"

"This virtue I stole," he said, leaning forward, "where was it when we were in Corfu? Virginity I remember. But I sort of remember you flinging it at me. I don't really remember me stealing it."

She sniffed. "What. Ever. The thing is that I'm not really sure what's in this for you and that makes me nervous. I've removed a couple of carrots and yet here you are still, like there's another treat for you to catch—and I'm concerned about exactly what treats you think you're going to be…getting from me. Because none. The answer is none."

"I want my child," he said, setting his wine glass down, his palms flat on the table. "Because I know how the world is. Because I know what it's like to grow up without a father. I know what it is to look at trees making shadows on your wall, and to not simply wonder what sort of evil things a bogeyman might do to you, but to know, with utter certainty, every horrible thing that could become of you. What it is to know that if the bogeyman ever did come there would be no one to protect you. My child will never know these fears. I will protect him. I will give him shelter with me, security. When I'm there, he will never worry. Not about one thing."

She looked down at the table and a plate of fish and rice was placed in front of her. It didn't look appetizing in the least. Her stomach was too full of knots and anxiety for her to take a bite of anything.

And Alex's speech had only added to the knots. She didn't

want to see the good in him. It was far too dangerous. She wanted to be angry. To look at him and see a mustache-twirling villain bent on tying her to the tracks in an attempt to defeat Ajax, who she was still trying to place in the position of hero.

Not that she could believe that Ajax was a villain, not in the least, but…but it wasn't like she was longing for him to ride in on his white horse, either.

"That's really good of you, Alex."

"It's basic human decency," he said. "Every parent should want to be there for their child. What about you, Rachel? Were your parents there for you?"

"Yes," she said. "Always. My father has always been involved in my and my sister's lives, and when Ajax came… He loves Ajax like a son. And so did my mother."

"You said your mother died?"

"A few years ago. She was ill. That's one reason I never went on to higher education or anything. I had to help. Leah was young and…and she needed to live her life. My mother wasn't the easiest person for me to get along with, but she was sick and she needed someone. So I can't possibly resent that I spent that time with her." She fiddled with her fork. "But then…well, then Ajax expressed the desire that we might…"

"Why did you put him off for so long?"

"I can see now, clear as day, that my saying I wanted to 'live a little' first was mainly because I just didn't feel anything for him. I dated some other men, but didn't have serious relationships with them because even though I knew Ajax wasn't putting an exclusive claim on me it felt like I would have been cheating." And she'd felt far too burned out to go there, but she wasn't going to bring that up. "And then we made it official and we've been engaged for years and…it was comfortable. To wear his ring and go on with life like it hadn't changed." She looked into her water glass. "And now *everything's* changed."

"Well, not everything. You aren't married."

"And I'm not going to be."

"Because you don't trust me?"

"There's that, but there's the fact that this isn't even close to being about trust. My father has promised ownership of Holt to the daughter who marries first and to the man she marries. He won't go back on a promise."

"Refreshing," Alex said, a dark light in his blue eyes.

"Yes, well, you don't get to benefit from it. Sorry."

"Too bad."

"I'm exhausted," she said, standing. "I think dinner wasn't the best idea. I'm going to my room."

"Fine. Shall I have your plate cleared?"

"Yes," she said. "And have cookies sent to my room. And decaf coffee. I don't want to eat healthy."

He arched a brow. "You are a rebel, Rachel Holt. How did the media ever paint you as anything else?"

"Shut up, Alex." She turned and walked back into the house, stalking to her room. She flung open the door and then slammed it with equal fervor.

She needed something. She needed…cookies. And to open a window so that she could breathe. She walked over to the other side of the room and flung the curtains open, then shoved the windows wide.

The breeze coming in off the ocean didn't help relieve the pressure in her chest. It didn't help anything.

She felt like she was going to burst. The pressure behind her eyes was so intense she could barely stand it.

But there was no release. She had worked so long to keep her emotions, her desires, anything too wild or demonstrative in check, that she couldn't let it out even now.

She couldn't even be herself when she was alone.

The scary thing was, she was pretty sure the only time

she'd been herself for more than a decade was during the night she'd spent in Alex's arms. Naked in every single way.

He hadn't deserved that. It had been a lie for him.

She took a deep breath, gulping the air down like water. She squeezed her eyes shut, hoping for tears, desperate for a crack in the foundations she'd built.

Nothing came.

Damn that Alex. She was so angry at him, so hurt by everything he'd done. And still she craved those moments of release, those moments of feeling like she was home in herself, that only he'd ever given her.

Well, that was too bad. She wasn't ever going to be back in his arms, ever again.

So she would just have to deal with that.

He married me, BTW.

Rachel stared down at the text from her sister, her body numb. She'd married Ajax? *Leah* had married *Ajax?*

When she'd started texting with Leah that morning she hadn't expected this. Leah had been checking on her, and she could get why, because running off like this was out of character for her, and because, yeah, she had a feeling they knew full well who Alex was.

But to find out Leah and Ajax had married? She didn't even know how to process that.

She got up from her position on the floor and went to her computer, typing in Ajax Kouros as quickly as she could.

And sure enough.

Ajax Kouros Weds Replacement Bride

"Well…wow."

She picked up the phone and typed in Holy crap. Just Googled.

You're happy? You didn't love Ajax did you?

Her sister's response came quickly. Leave it to Leah to worry about her, even still. Rachel couldn't imagine her sweet younger sister with Ajax. Hell, *she* was the one who was worried.

As for the love part...

Not like that. Not the kind you need to marry a guy. You know?

She hit Send. It was a lie of omission in a lot of ways. Because she would have married him. If things hadn't changed. If not for the baby.

The baby. All of this kept hitting her in little pieces. She had a feeling if it hit her all at once she would be completely buried by it.

Do you love Alex?

Her sister's message hit her right in the chest. Because it brought her back to that night. To those feelings. Feelings that were so different from anything she'd ever experienced before.

I need to be with Alex.

She typed it, but didn't hit Send right away. It was the truth. She had to figure out how they were going to make this work, what they were going to do.

She'd stayed up half the night reading, browsing the internet and eating cookies and basically trying to figure out what had gone wrong in her world and how she was going to fix it.

She knew one thing for sure: That she had to give Alex

a chance to be in his child's life. Beyond that? She had no clue.

She finished out her conversation with Leah and tossed her phone down onto the bed.

Oh, great. And there went her line of defense. Her "No, Alex, you villain! I cannot marry you!" was going to be so much weaker now.

Although, it was nice to know that Holt was secure. That it would still go to Ajax, because even though she hadn't wanted to marry him, she hadn't wanted him to lose anything, either.

But Leah... Oh, she hoped Leah would be happy. That she knew what she was doing. Leah had always been fond of Ajax. They'd always gotten along, but she hadn't gotten the idea that her sister wanted to marry him.

Maybe she was wrong. Maybe they were both better at hiding who they were than people realized. Rachel was sure her sister would never believe that she was a bad girl living inside of a good girl, and that both entities had a penchant for cookies. That she'd had a one-night stand on vacation with her fiancé's enemy. Nope. She was sure no one would guess that.

There was a knock on the bedroom door, and this one, she guessed, was Alex. Though she was a little shocked the man knew how to observe things like knocking. It was a social nicety she wouldn't have credited him with.

"Come in," she said, straightening and hoping she didn't look like she'd had an all-night cookie and internet bender, even though she had.

Alex strode into the room, as usual, his charisma filling up the small space in a way that was shocking.

"They got married," he said.

"So I saw," she returned, and she was sure they were talking about the same people.

"Are you okay?" he asked. It was shockingly sensitive,

all things considered. A lot more sensitive than a man who was just out to use her should ever be.

"I'm…fine. Worried about Leah. I didn't want her to… to marry someone she didn't love for me."

"Maybe it wasn't for you."

"Of course it was," she said.

"The whole world doesn't revolve around you, you know."

"No, I'm well aware of that. I get used a lot. But what I want doesn't ever seem to be that important."

"Are you sorry you aren't married to him?"

"Am I sorry that I'm not trapped in a loveless marriage with him?"

"You could be trapped in one with me," he said. "It might take your mind off her."

"Nice try, but I actually think that I might relish my newfound freedom."

"What do you mean?"

"I have screwed everything up. When the press find out…well, when the press find out, I'm not going to be their princess anymore. They love me, sure, but they love Ajax and the wayward woman will always be the villain. My father will be so disappointed that I…that I didn't learn. Leah's had to marry someone she doesn't love because of me. I've messed up everything. I have…no reason at all, in all the world, to keep doing what's expected of me. Or rather to start again. I'm ruined," she said, laughing. "Utterly ruined. And there's no point even trying to backpedal. To try and legitimize myself by marrying my baby's father when it won't change the circumstances. My father can't pay anyone off and make this go away."

"So you're ready to go and face the press then?"

"I am absolutely not," she said. "I…I want you to know that no matter what…whether I was pregnant or not, press or not, whether you had come or not…I wasn't going to marry him."

"Is that the case?" he asked, his voice rough.

"Yes. I can't. I…I can't. But that doesn't make me brave. I would still be hiding, without the baby. I'm a coward, and I feel totally fragile and I want to hide out for a while and figure out…what all *this* means. See what…what happens with the pregnancy."

"Do you have any reason to believe you'll miscarry?" he asked. He looked disturbed by the idea, which was strangely touching. It was easy to imagine he was digging in and doing the right thing because of his past experience, but he almost seemed to want the baby. Almost seemed like he would be sorry now if it didn't happen.

And she felt a little bit shocked by the revelation that she would be sad if something happened. That she wanted the baby, no matter the circumstances.

"No. Not any reason beyond statistics. I mean…they happen, don't they?"

"I suppose. But it hardly seems right to plan for one."

"I'm not. I'm just being cautious."

"I have to go back to New York for the work week. I have several clients I need to meet with and it has to be done in person."

"Why can't you Skype them or something?"

He leaned against the door frame, arms crossed over his broad chest. "I'm new in town still. Comparatively. That means I have to play by other people's rules sometimes."

"You must hate that."

He smiled that wicked, enticing smile. "I hate rules. But you have to play the game. And the game has been good to me so far. It's how I've earned my money. It's how a kid from a brothel ended up being a billionaire."

"Well, have fun in New York," she said. She didn't want

to probe deeper. Didn't want to find out more about him. Didn't want him to seem so human.

"You aren't going to come?"

"Was I invited?"

"Of course. You want to stay here then?"

She did, weirdly. She should go home and face the music. Her father. Everything. But she wasn't ready for that yet. She wasn't ready to share her and Alex's...*relationship?* Whatever it was, with her family. When she told her family she was pregnant, she would have to confess that she'd had that little indiscretion and she wasn't ready to tell them yet.

Wasn't ready to expose that part of herself, a part she'd only just discovered. A part Alex had uncovered.

She hadn't even known she was capable of being swept away on a tide of desire, and she wasn't really ready to let anyone else in on her revelation.

"Yes."

"By yourself?" he asked.

"Sounds ideal, actually."

He pushed off from the door frame. "Well then, please yourself."

"Shall."

"I will see you next week."

She nodded slowly. "Okay. Next week, then."

"Then...then we'll decide what we're going to do."

She nodded, holding back a groan. She wasn't ready to decide anything.

"No guarantees."

"People do not tell me no, Rachel. I warn you of that right now."

"Funny, I've told you no quite a few times."

"Yes. But before you said no, you said yes. Pretty emphatically. I'm sure I can get you to say it again."

CHAPTER SEVEN

HE WAS SO TIRED he wanted to lie down and not get up for three days. But he didn't want to lie down alone. He wanted to lie down next to Rachel. To pull her curvy body against his and just hold her while he slept.

That was probably the jet lag talking, but oh, well.

It was morning on the island, late night in New York. What he had to do was drink an espresso and suck it up. He was young—there were plenty of people his age who partied every night and went to work the next morning.

For some reason, though, half the time he felt old.

Maybe it was the strain of being a respectable business-man when he knew that it just wasn't programmed into him genetically. He would have been better off selling his body for cash or selling other people to turn a profit.

He shut down that line of thinking and walked into the house.

He could hear singing. Coming from the kitchen. It was off-key, and it was horrible. Warbling about wanting to make someone feel wanted.

He followed the noise like a bread crumb trail, and at the end of it was a blonde with her hair piled high on her head in a messy bun, dancing around the room in short pajama shorts with an empty mug in her hand.

"Good morning," he said. "Is the coffee made?"

She stopped then flailed, her arms flung wide. "Ack!"

"Sorry to interrupt."

"You scared me. I didn't know when you'd be back."

"I texted you." That was how he'd kept in touch with her over the past week. The occasional text just to make sure she was okay. Sometimes she'd even responded without an insult.

"I hadn't checked my phone yet."

"I'm so disappointed you weren't waiting for contact from me with bated breath."

"Sorry." She went over to the coffeemaker and set about filling the empty mug.

"Thank you," he said.

"It's for me."

He shot her his deadliest look and went to the cabinet and picked out his own mug, then poured himself a cup. "I don't think you appreciate how much I need the caffeine."

"I'm supposed to limit it, but I can't seem to shake the need for an early morning cup. But the doctor said that was okay."

"Doctor?"

"Yes. I managed to secure myself a covert doctor visit while you were gone."

He leaned against the counter. "And?"

"Knocked up, as we thought."

"And?"

"It's early. No point doing an ultrasound or anything like that."

"But everything is fine. And you can drink a coffee."

She curled her fingers like talons around her mug, her eyes glittering evilly. "I can drink a coffee."

"Okay. Don't cut me or anything."

"Hiss."

"You just said hiss."

"Hissing at you would be overdramatic. It was like a pre-hiss. A warning."

He looked at her, in her pajamas, her feet bare, toenails bright pink, her hair piled high on her head, and laughed. She was the most absurd little thing he'd ever encountered.

"What?" she asked.

"You're so weird."

"I am?"

"Yes."

"Why are you shocked by it?"

He shrugged. "The press makes you look like some... staid and stable ribbon-cutter."

"Ribbon-cutter?"

"Like you go to openings and stand there and cut the ribbon."

"Hmph. That's your bad for believing the media's representation of me! They only see a small bit of who I am, and they report on a piece of that. They don't know me or what I do at home."

"Is that their fault or yours?"

"What does that mean?"

"You're very guarded, Rachel, and while I have to say you don't seem to be around me, in general, I think you are. Does anyone know you?"

Rachel paused with her coffee mug halfway to her lips. She was unhappy because seeing Alex walk into the kitchen had sent her heart way up into her throat, even worse than it had done when he'd sent her text messages during the time he'd been away.

"Alana probably a little."

"Alana?"

"My friend. The one I was in Corfu with. The one who encouraged me to go and talk to you. She was my maid of honor along with Leah, actually. Well, she would have been had I gone through with the wedding."

"And she knows you?"

She winced. "Mostly." Alana had been there for the wild

past. They'd passed a liquor bottle back and forth between them in her Mercedes. They'd cleaned up their act together. But Alana didn't know that Rachel felt like she was suffocating beneath her skin.

She shopped with Alana, she talked shallow crap with Alana. She and Leah had warm chats where Rachel felt obligated to seem stable and to give advice. She and her father had a similar relationship. She always felt like she needed to seem happy, so that he wouldn't worry that something was wrong again. That she might be sliding back into her old ways.

Then there was Ajax…and with him she had to be… well, calm and fine and…and…things. With Ajax she was the woman she pretended to be for the media. Poised and steady. She could never do anything that might point in the direction of her very covered up, fairly sordid teenage years. She could never flail or cuss.

She did both of those things around Alex. With alarming frequency. And she wasn't sure why. Maybe because he'd seen her naked. Or maybe because she'd been naked since she met him. Metaphorically.

"I've just never… Everyone has their expectations. And what they need from me. You, on the other hand, well, I don't need to be a certain way around you because I don't even like you, and also we're stuck together, so what you think about me or want from me doesn't really matter."

His eyes went blank. "I don't really know what it's like to have someone have expectations of you."

"Oh. Well, it's not bad. I don't really mind it or anything. It's just that…it means that I make sure I behave a certain way in certain company is all. And yeah, I don't go around saying weird things in public or around people who wouldn't get it. So I'm…restrained in certain settings and…"

"Fake," he said.

"What?"

"You're fake. And that's okay, I am, too. I mean, I know how to be. Witness how we met. And how do you think I survive a week of meetings like this? I don't go in telling them where I'm from. I make sure to temper my language. I've learned how to dress in a way that reflects who I am now, and what I do now, not in a way that reflects who I was. Or where I'm from."

"I'm not fake."

"Don't look so upset."

She realized she was frowning with great ferocity. She didn't bother to stop. "How can I not be upset when you're telling me that I'm fake?"

"Because it's a life skill. Chameleons do it. It's how they survive. It's how *we* survive. You don't want to walk around showing the wrong colors, so to speak. You have to learn how to blend in."

"Deep, man."

"It's the truth is all. And you do it, so you obviously, instinctively, know the benefits of it, whether you like it or not."

"It's…being appropriate in your surroundings. It's not fake."

"Is it authentic?"

"Does it… What does that mean?"

"I'm not judging you, Rachel, I'm observing."

Her phone started buzzing against the hard marble tile and she grabbed it, looking at the screen with no small amount of dread. Because she hadn't talked to Ajax at all since his wedding with Leah and she hadn't talked to Leah on the phone. Or her father. And she didn't know if she could handle any of them.

Fortunately the caller ID showed that it was Alana. Alana, who she was prepared to deal with at least. They'd talked a little bit during the week, and while she hadn't broken the pregnancy news, her friend had guessed that Alex was the reason for the wedding no-show and had been nothing but supportive.

"I have to take this. In an authentic manner." She hit the green button on the screen. "Hi. What?"

Alana was talking so fast that Rachel could hardly decode what she was saying. "A huge order. Like…huge, and I can't fulfill it if I can't buy the materials—I'm only getting half paid up front. And you're not even going to believe this! A pipe burst in the shop upstairs and flooded me completely. I have ruined inventory, things that I can't just replace and my insurance thinks her insurance is responsible and vice versa and it's just absolute madness!"

"What can I do?"

"There's the obvious but I hesitate to ask."

"Well, since I'm part owner in the business, it makes sense that I help, especially since— What is this huge order?"

"It's costume stuff, which I don't love to do, but I'd get a film credit. It's for a really big French film and—"

"Say no more. I'm coming over. We'll get it all worked out."

"You don't have to come if you're still deep in issues with your mystery man."

Rachel looked up at Alex. "Let me worry about that." She hung up. "I have to go to Cannes."

"What?"

"My friend Alana has a boutique there. Technically, *I* have a boutique there. I own most of it. But I'm a silent business partner, as it were."

"How is it I didn't know that?"

"No one knows that," she said. "Not even Ajax. And yes, I felt a little guilty about it, but I believe in her skills as a designer and I wanted to support her. So I set her up with a boutique. And we've been turning a decent profit the past few years. She's having a crisis now, though—burst pipe upstairs—and we have damaged clothes. So I need to go and see what all happened, and try to help her get everything put back together."

"That's easy," he said. "Throw money at it."

"What? Like just pay someone to go and fix it all?"

"Why not?"

"I have a budget. What? I do. I have a trust, yes, but I have to live off of it. And I just stopped living in the apartment my father paid for. And I've just burned some bridges, so all things considered, I should throw a mop at it, not money. It needs to get done quickly because she has a chance to pick up a major client, but not if she's underwater. So to speak."

"I could pay for it. You know, if you were my wife I would feel obligated to pay for it."

"Oh, no! I'm not your wife, though. I'm not even your fiancée. You know what? It feels really good not to be someone's fiancée. It really does."

"I'm happy for you."

"You don't sound it. So anyway, as I'm assuming I'm not a prisoner, I need to get a plane off this island and get myself to Cannes."

"Are you coming back?"

She bit her lip. "I don't know. I might stay with Alana for a while. This, you and me, is probably going to end in shared custody."

He frowned. "That's not how I want it to end."

"How do you see this ending?"

"With our family together. You with your child, me with both of you. You in my bed."

She choked on her coffee, coughing and sputtering, bracing herself on the counter until she could suck in a breath that wasn't blocked by liquid. "What?" she finally managed to rasp.

"What did you think I meant when I proposed marriage?"

"Something not so…intimate."

"And why not? We're good together, *agape*."

"Whatever. You only slept with me because you were being revenge-y. And you were wanting to steal Ajax's woman and his business and whatever. It had nothing to do with me."

A muscle in his jaw ticked. "I suppose. But things have changed. You're the mother of my child and all things considered…"

"I will never be a convenience. Not for any man. Not ever again. You talked about being fake. Fine, maybe I've been fake. I didn't even know it, though. That's the thing. I didn't know…how far from love what I felt for Ajax was, and I'll never put myself in that position just to make other people comfortable. I'm done making other people comfortable. I'm going to make me and my baby comfortable. Beginning and end of story."

"Well, then, I suppose I should drink more coffee and pack."

"Why?"

"Because, apparently, we're going to Cannes."

"We?"

"I'm not done with you, Rachel. Not by a long shot. And hey, this time, I'll pay for the hotel room. Since you paid for the last one."

Her ears burned. "Did you not just hear what I said?" She really needed him to not be suggesting they pick up where they left off in Corfu, because she was genuinely afraid that she would be too weak to tell him no. That she would say "yes, yes, take me!" and lie down on the nearest flat surface so he could have his wicked way with her, and that would accomplish nothing.

It would be fun, though…

Maybe. But she wasn't going to have any more of that kind of fun with him. She had, in some strange way, been set free by all these crazy turns of events, and she was going to make the most of that freedom. Not head toward another loveless engagement.

"I heard you. I'll get us a penthouse suite with separate bedrooms. It will be very luxurious and private and it will not interfere with your budget."

"Well...thanks. But why?"

"Because I am not going to give up on you, *agape mou*. On us."

"Because you love me so much?" she asked, her heart hammering, her palms sweaty. She'd asked it to put him off. To mock him. Instead, she found herself standing there shaking, a part of her praying his answer would be yes.

"Not at all. Love isn't in the cards for a man like me, Rachel. I wouldn't even know where to begin. But a family... I thought I would like to try."

She swallowed hard. "But I need more than that, Alex. I need more than just you trying. I'm not going to be your happy family experiment, it's not fair."

"You don't have a happy family, experimental or otherwise at the moment, so why not?"

She tried to ignore the punch to the gut his words delivered. But it was impossible. Because she'd lived the past eleven years holding her family together. Being what they needed. And now it was gone.

It was gone and she didn't know what to do without it.

It was like realizing that pieces of her armor had been stripped away. Threatening to expose her. Vulnerable. So soft and easily hurt.

She crossed her arms beneath her breasts, as if that might hold what was left of her armor close to her skin. As if it might protect her.

Suddenly she was very aware of the baby inside of her,

and that, in spite of the fact she had a human in her, she'd never felt so alone or frightened in all of her life. As if everything, inside and out, had turned completely alien.

She would take pictures of herself being intimate with her former almost-lover hitting the news any day over the feeling that had grabbed her by the throat just now.

"I...I need to go," she said. "Send the plane. I'll pack."

"No. Lucy will pack for you. You rest here and I will see to all the arrangements." For Alex, he seemed almost contrite.

"You don't have to come."

"You don't want me to?" he asked.

"No."

"You can't always get what you want, *agape*."

CHAPTER EIGHT

"Show-off," she said, looking around the penthouse and walking toward the window, looking out at the ocean below.

The flight to Cannes had been quick and uneventful. The uneventful part he credited to the fact that Rachel had ignored him the entire time.

"What? The hotel room you put me up in was very nice. And the room service was excellent."

Something flashed in her eyes that he didn't like. Pain. Shame. "You aren't authorized to joke about that night," she said. "I don't like the reminder that you used me."

"No more than you used me. You were engaged to another man, after all. You were hardly blameless."

"You knew, though. I didn't trick you."

"Can we not have this fight again? The one where you tell me all the things I did to wound you? I felt...guilty, after it happened, Rachel. That's why I didn't call. That's why I didn't storm your wedding. It's why I came to see you and not him."

She frowned. "You felt guilty."

"It turns out that when you seek revenge on someone you hate...because of the way they treated women—the way they treated people in general—and you use someone in order to do it, you come out feeling a lot like the thing you despise."

It was the truth. He'd never allowed himself to fully

form the thought. To examine exactly why the whole incident with her left him feeling dirty. Empty. It was because it was another piece of evidence for the trial being conducted over his soul.

Innocent or guilty. Victim or predator. Which was he?

He didn't even know the answer. And it burned.

"A conscience, huh?" she asked.

"I'm maybe not as bad as you think. I'm maybe not as good as I think, but…also perhaps I'm not completely amoral, either. Which is good to know."

"Do you want to be…good?"

He frowned. "I don't know. I know what I don't want to be."

"So you really… You really think you grew up in a brothel with Ajax."

"I did," he said, his chest tightening. "He wouldn't remember me. I was a boy when he left. Maybe eight. But I remember him. And his father."

A leaden weight settled in his chest. As it did whenever he thought too much about…everything. When he had moments of wanting to call Ajax's father "my father."

He swallowed past the bile that was rising in his throat. *Bad blood, right? That's the way it works.*

It must. Except it didn't seem to work that way for Ajax. Ajax, who'd acquired a family when he'd left the compound. Ajax, who'd had no trouble finding love.

He couldn't think about it. It gave him a headache. It was too complicated. Too hard.

"He never told me about his life before he came to work for my family," she said. "I mean…nothing. He never said a thing about it and now…now I think it's a bit strange. But honestly, Alex, if you knew him…he's so serious. He never does one thing out of line. I can't even imagine the man you're describing."

"He was little better than a boy," Alex said, his voice

rough. "I suppose I imagined he hadn't changed much as a man. That when I met you you would have stories of him in excess, and that he would be the same."

"He doesn't even drink. He's the most outrageously decent man I've ever known, and no, he doesn't inspire great passion in me. But he's a friend. He's not a bad person."

"But he was," Alex said, feeling the need to justify himself. "He was."

"Or maybe he just had his moments? Like you said, what happened with me…it wasn't your best."

"No," he said.

"It wasn't mine, either. But I don't think it was my worst. Well, it depends on how you look at it. It wasn't the worst thing that's ever happened to me. It was definitely the worst thing I've done. Because I didn't keep my promises, and that was… That wasn't right of me."

"What was the worst thing?" he asked, his throat getting so tight he could scarcely breathe.

"I don't want to talk about it. Actually, what I should do is run and check on Alana."

"I'll go with you."

"You don't need to."

"I want to. I want to be a part of your life. And I'm frustrated because I'm not really sure how to accomplish that beyond lying to you."

A crease dented her forehead. "What would you say?"

"What?"

"If you were going to lie to try and keep me in your life, what would you say?"

He looked at her, at her flawless face and the deep blue eyes that carried a wealth of depth and hurt behind them. Hurt he didn't want to add to, even though he knew he already had.

"I would tell you that I loved you. That my life would

be nothing without you. That I needed you. More than my next breath."

Her blue eyes shimmered, tears pooling in them and he wished for a second that what he said could be true. But he didn't know how to feel those things.

And even if he could...

He would never risk them.

For some reason that resolution pushed forward an image of a baby. A squalling, delicate newborn whose cries screamed need. Need for him.

It made his chest feel strange. Tight and heavy. A strange sort of helplessness crept around the edges. The kind he hadn't felt since he was a boy, surrounded by evil he knew he could never combat.

And the people who should have been protecting them— protecting him—they were the monsters.

There was no hopelessness deeper than that. And he'd felt it every day, a feeling that had only intensified the day he'd learned the truth. The day he'd run.

And now you're going to be a father.

The thought was enough to buckle his knees. To send him straight to the ground.

"Well," she said, bursting through the haze of his thoughts, "that would certainly be dramatic." She swallowed visibly. "And of course I wouldn't believe you."

"Wise. That's what you call learning from your mistakes."

She flinched. "I suppose so. Now, I'm going to go and deal with Alana's crisis. Alone, actually. Yes, I'm going alone, so find something to amuse yourself."

"Did you just tell me to amuse myself?"

"Yeah. I can give you some spending money if you like."

He frowned. "You need it more than I do. But your attempts at flippancy over the past week have been amusing. If flawed."

"As have been your attempts at being a decent human being. All right. I'm going."

"Where is her shop?"

"I'll text you."

"And I'll find it. When should I expect you back?" he asked, crossing his arms over his chest.

"When I'm back."

"So I won't know if you've been backed into an alley by the paparazzi or if you're just running late? That doesn't work for me. Estimate a time or at least give me your location."

"Are you...worried about me?"

"The baby," he bit out, the word making his stomach ache.

"Well, of course. That's what I meant."

"Yes," he said.

"Thanks. I'm... Thank you. I'm going to go. I'll be back here by seven. If I'm not, I'll text you."

He nodded and watched her walk back out of the room, his stomach flipping over itself. Maybe he should be thankful for her refusal to marry him. What did he know about being a father? What did he know about being a husband?

All he knew was that he felt a need to be close to her. To protect her. And he knew, with a total certainty, that he would feel that way about the baby.

He meant to offer them protection. But he had no idea who would protect them from him. No, he would never harm them with his hands. But...

He had always pictured Ajax's veins being filled with black poison. When he'd been a boy and he or Nikola would walk past him, it was a strong vision he'd had. That they were something different than men. That if you cut them, evil would pour out. They exuded it. How could it not be a physical thing beneath their skin?

And then he'd found out the truth.

If their blood was black, then his was, too.

Because it was the same blood.

Worse, he'd seen Ajax lose that legacy. Had seen him walk away and create a new life. He'd seen his mother, desperate to cling to the man she'd loved.

The men he'd always considered evil seemed to have no trouble binding people to them.

The same legacy had been coursing through his veins since birth, and yet no one had ever chosen to stay with him.

It made him fear that the only thing he'd inherited was the darkness.

The skin on Rachel's arms prickled as a breeze blew across the water and over her. She and Alana had just closed up shop after assessing the damage, and Alana had gone with her boyfriend back to their apartment.

Rachel had just been standing out in front of the store, looking across the harbor at the yachts, at where blue sky met blue water, rich colors fading together.

She breathed in deep and the breeze set the hair on the back of her neck on end and brushed a tingling sensation over her, down to her fingertips. It wasn't fear. But it was something she couldn't ignore. Something urgent, little bursts of it popping through her until she turned her head.

And then it all made sense.

Alex was walking toward her, hands in his pockets. He was dressed casually, nothing like he'd been that day on the yacht, but still much more relaxed than Alex the Businessman. A pale blue shirt open at the collar and a pair of dark jeans.

"I'm glad to see you've not been buried beneath photographers."

"Oh, well, thank heaven for the off-season. None of the locals would dare break their cool by raising an eyebrow at my presence, much less interrupt their day by setting the paparazzi on me."

"Thank God for people far too blasé to care for a bit of scandal."

She laughed. "I suppose."

The moment was strange. Like that time a month ago in Greece playing over again. Different setting, different time. But the pull was there. Whether she wanted it to be or not, it was there. Engagement ring or not, it had been there. Conniving plot to seduce her to get revenge on Ajax or not, it had been there.

Even now, with the baby and all the baggage, it was there.

She knew he felt it, too. She could see it in those wicked blue eyes. He was thinking of sex and sin and all the wonderful things they'd done together. She didn't know how she knew it, only that she did. Only that for some reason she had a connection with him that she couldn't explain. One she didn't want at all.

Why couldn't he just be that jerk who'd seduced her? Or, if she couldn't summon up the rage to think of him as a jerk, why couldn't he just be the cause of her pregnancy? A distant figure until they had to work out a shared custody agreement? It's not like he could do anything for her now anyway.

But there was more. She hated that there was more, but there was. This deep, sexual connection that somehow felt like…more. Why did it keep going with him? Why, no matter the depth of feeling she was willing to admit she had with him, did a small voice inside of her keep whispering *it's more?*

Stupid small voice inside of her.

"Dinner?" he asked, another echo from the past.

"Yes." She felt the yes slip off her lips and a deep ache

slide down deep inside of her. Her body responding to the consent.

For dinner, you little hussy. Dinner. Down, girl.

He held his hand out, and she didn't take it. Because if she did, she knew she was really, really sunk. She had no business touching him. No business even flirting with the idea of engaging in intimacy with him again.

The fact that he was a lying liar aside, they had too much going on to confuse it all with more sex.

As if things could get more confused, but whatever.

"Where are we having dinner?" she asked. Because it seemed to her they were just going back toward the hotel.

"I hate to see a perfectly good terrace wasted, so I thought we would dine at the suite."

"You make it sound so fancy."

"It is," he said. "It's very fancy. And dinner should be waiting for us already. And I will be having juice, along with you."

"That's…well, that's awfully sensitive of you."

"You sound surprised."

"I am," she said, walking next to him, acutely aware of the way they both held their arms at their sides as they walked. Acutely aware of how they weren't touching when their fingertips were so close.

That wasn't how it was supposed to work. She was supposed to not touch him and have all the attraction magically resolve. Her shell was supposed to protect her. All those years of self-denial. Of never letting her passion out. Learning to be risk-averse, learning to keep every emotion, every desire, every need shoved down deep and covered by a layer of smooth, impenetrable steel. All of that should have helped her now. Should have preserved her.

But it wasn't and she couldn't understand it. How eleven years of hard-won control had just suddenly melted as if it had never been there in the first place.

They walked into the hotel in total silence, then took the elevator to their floor. The double doors to the terrace were open, a wash of pink evening light painting the living area.

She walked through the suite and outside. The table was set for two, a bottle of sparkling grape juice in an ice bucket, wrapped in a linen towel as if it were fine champagne. And their plates were covered with a silver dome, everything set and ready.

As though Alex had wanted to make sure they weren't disturbed.

"This is romantic," she said, her tone about as dry as sand.

"Is it?" he looked around as though the notion surprised him. "I just asked for dinner for two and that we not be disturbed. For privacy's sake, as we are discussing personal matters and you are a bit of a public figure. Romance never came into it."

"Naturally not. Come to think of it, you aren't much of a romantic, are you?"

He shook his head. "I've never had much practice with it. But I would like to think I romanced you that night we were together."

"You seduced me. Completely different. I wasn't looking for romance."

"So you were looking for sex?"

"No," she said. "But I think that's why it worked."

She sat down and grabbed the bottle out of the bucket, eyeing the cork warily. "It has a cork."

"Yes."

"These things freak me out. You do it." She handed him the bottle and he took it, working the metal cage off the cork so that it popped up. She winced at the sound. "Gah. I always expect it to fly out and poke someone in the eye."

He laughed. "Not likely. But then, caution isn't a bad thing."

"That's certainly been my motto in life."

He arched a brow as he poured her a glass of the sparkling juice.

"It has been. For…a while. Because…because bad things happen to you when you put yourself out there, you know?"

He nodded slowly. "No," he said, the words at odds with the gesture. "I don't. Because I never put myself out there."

"So you never have girlfriends, do you?"

"No. One-night-stand stuff. Sometimes women who hang around for a couple of weekends. Nothing more than that."

Strangely, it didn't really bother her to hear him say that. She would have been more disturbed in some ways if there had been a woman in his life that he loved.

And she really didn't want to know why that was.

Silly since she'd been in love before. Even if it had turned out badly. Sillier still because she didn't love Alex and she didn't want him to love her, either. But nothing about her feelings for him were logic-centered. None at all.

"That seems smart," she said. "I mean, in some ways. It wouldn't really work for me, I bet, because the guys would go to the press." She hadn't meant to tread that close to the truth of her past.

"It must be inconvenient. For my part, as rich as I am, only financial magazines seem to care."

"It surprises me because your face would sell magazines."

"I'm content out of the spotlight."

Her heart bumped into her breastbone. "If you're seen with me…I mean, when people find out…you'll be in the spotlight. You know that, right? Your anonymity is sort of over."

"I can deal with that," he said, pulling the covers off of their dinner to reveal some sort of fish dish. It had crispy skin. And a head. Oh, Lord, it had a head. She didn't mind fish, usually, but after spending so much time in Greece and then on his island, she was concerned she was going to grow gills.

"I love the sea," she said. "I'm underwhelmed by seafood, to be honest." She poked at it with her fork. "Daaaaang. It has a head."

He laughed at her, then bent across the table and took her plate, and his, and put them back by a nearby tray. "Hold that thought."

He went back into the hotel room and she couldn't help but watch his butt as he went. She looked away and back down into her drink and she didn't realize he'd returned until he spoke. "I ordered a pizza. What's the point of all this pretension?"

She laughed. "A pizza?"

"I was promised it would be here in ten minutes."

"Tell me there are no anchovies on it, because if there are, we haven't solved any of my problems."

"No anchovies. Promise."

"Good. What did you get?"

"Pineapple."

"I love!"

"Me, too."

A strange sort of calm settled between them, and it felt more disturbing than the tension from earlier. This wasn't like it had been a month ago. Not entirely. There was an edge of comfort, of domesticity to this that hit a nerve in her.

They tried to make clumsy small talk until they heard the knock at the door and he went off for the pizza, setting the box on their table.

She laughed. "So much for romance."

He shrugged. "This is better. It's real, anyway."

"True." She flipped up the lid on the box and took out a piece of pizza, chewing through the burn of the first bite.

Worth the pain to get the cheese at the optimum point. "So," she said, after she swallowed. "Do you get pizza often?"

He looked down, then back up, and she was hit, once again, with the full impact of his beauty. "Do you want to know a secret?" he asked.

"Yes."

He leaned in, the look in his eyes intent. "After I left my…the compound, I didn't have any money. So I slept where I could and ate what I could, and I still felt better about it because I wasn't a part of that horrible place."

"I can understand that."

"But once I started making money, and I got my own apartment…I didn't want to buy filet mignon or lobster. I'd had all that. Living in that house… It was the darkest pieces of glamor and excess. Junkies throwing up in the halls, people having sex in public. But then we'd sit down to some formal dinner like this insane family or something. Anyway, I never wanted to revisit that. I'd never just had a pizza. I ordered it almost every night for a…a long time."

He looked down and took a bite of pizza, the gestures and expressions boyish now. It was strange; sometimes he seemed so young. Sometimes he seemed about a thousand years old. And she could relate, because sometimes that was exactly how she felt, too. Too young, too old and never just right.

"What did you have on the first one?"

"The pizza?"

"Yeah," she said, her stomach tight. "I'm sure you remember."

The left corner of his mouth quirked upward. "Yeah. Pepperoni. Black olives. It was New York style. Of course, at the time I'd only dreamed of New York. I live there now. The pizza's much better than this."

She laughed. "Yeah, I know. I spent at least half my childhood there. Most of my adult life. I've been fortunate to travel a lot from an early age."

"I barely left the Kouklakis compound until I was fourteen."

"What?"

"There was…nowhere else to go. And they didn't really want anyone talking to us. Questioning us. There weren't very many children. The ones that were there had to be careful. Careful to try and go unnoticed by anyone who might want to use us, people who came for parties and things. Careful about what we said. The wrong words could set the police down on Nikola and that would have been unforgivable. Death for certain."

"He would have killed…children?"

"He would never have gotten his own hands that dirty. But he would have used someone else's. I always knew that my life was in a tenuous place as long as I was there. I always knew." He took another bite of pizza. "But I got free. I got pizza. It has a happy ending, yes?"

"Does it?"

"What do you mean?"

"Well, it's not over yet. Right now we're just sitting here eating pizza. It's not going to fade to black or anything."

"True."

"There are a lot of potential outcomes for all of this. And I'm not sure if any of them are wildly happy."

He grunted, a short, frustrated sound seated in the back of his throat. "Because you're looking for something I can't give you. You could be happy if you just—"

"If I what?"

"—compromised. You were willing to do it for Ajax and you didn't even want him. You weren't having his baby. Well, you are having my baby, and you do want me, so I don't see any reason that you shouldn't want to marry me instead of him. What changed?"

She looked down. "I think I did. Or maybe I didn't change, maybe I just became more afraid of what might happen if I kept living my life as someone else, someone safe, and less afraid of what might happen if I made an effort to find some happiness."

"I think I made you pretty happy for extended periods of time in bed," he said.

She coughed. "Well, there's that."

"I want you, Rachel."

"What...now?" She looked around them, at the blue-tinged air slowly falling darker as the sun sank below the horizon line.

"Every moment since the first time I saw you. And that's not me lying to keep you here, that's me telling you the truth. That's me confessing. Frankly, I know this isn't going to get me anywhere with you so you have to believe that it's honest. Because I know that it doesn't mean anything to you that the moment I saw you, I forgot Ajax's name, and every thought I ever had about revenge. Because all I could think about was getting you naked then and there. Not romantic, maybe. But all I know is that it didn't matter then who you were. I mean...not in the sense of who you were to Ajax, or the media, or what your marriage had to do with him acquiring Holt. It only mattered...who you were. Which I know sounds stupid, but in my head it made sense."

Rachel's heart was pounding hard, echoing in her head. She leaned forward, grabbed his collar and tugged him to her, kissing him on the mouth. She didn't know what she was doing or why. Only that she couldn't stop.

And along with her heartbeat, his words reverberated through her. *It only mattered who you were.*

He cupped the back of her head and pulled her in harder, taking the kiss deeper, his tongue sliding against hers, sending a wave of lust down through her body. Nothing was settled. And she shouldn't be kissing him. Shouldn't be making things confusing by throwing a match on their simmering physical chemistry.

But he'd said he wanted her. And everything in her responded to that. It fought to break free, to push past the boundaries she'd placed around herself, a neat little fence that kept her safe and hidden.

Because he wanted that part of her. He didn't want her to hide it. Didn't want her to keep it behind a locked door. Didn't want her to keep her passion from him. And she wanted to give him that. Wanted to give it to herself, this moment of freedom. Another chance to grab it. To try and feel something.

She'd spent so long not feeling. This was like coming to the surface of the water and breathing in air, filling her aching lungs when she hadn't even realized what she'd been missing.

She hadn't realized how much pain had been caused by holding herself under. Because it had been a slow-growing pain, easier to deal with than the idea of having herself exposed to the media, of being used by a man she'd thought she loved.

Still, it hurt. And she was only now seeing just how much.

"I have garlic breath," she said when they parted, breathing hard and hoping it wasn't too offensive.

"I probably do, too."

"Well, I didn't notice so I guess we're good."

"Stop talking, Rachel."

She nodded. "It would be for the best."

She moved away from him and away from the table so it wasn't between them anymore. He rounded it, pulled her to him and kissed her like he was starving. She wrapped her arms around his neck, clung to him.

He tightened his hold on her, propelling her backward until she was pressed up against the rough stone wall of the hotel. "I need you," he said, kissing her cheek, her neck, her collarbone. "Rachel. *Theos,* how have I survived this long without touching you?"

She wanted to cry, and she wanted to come, and she couldn't figure out, in the end, which need would win out. It all felt too big for her, too much. Too much for a girl who was used to hiding in her shell, to feel stripped and exposed like this.

But she couldn't stop. She couldn't.

She pulled his shirt open, not caring that it scattered buttons everywhere, not caring that she could hear the sounds of traffic below, that they had nothing to cover them. She pushed his shirt off his shoulders and ran her hands over his chest, the hard muscles, the rough hair.

"You're so hot," she said.

"We've had this conversation before."

"I know, but I have to say it again because it's all I can think about when I see you. When I touch you. You make me... Alex, I don't understand this. I didn't think this was how I was. Not anymore. I thought it was gone."

He dipped low and kissed her, forcing her head against the wall, the hard surface behind her the only thing keeping her from melting into a puddle on the ground. One of his hands slid low, down to her thigh. His fingers dug into her skin, his grip tightening as he lifted her leg and held it up over his lower back, bracing her with his hand and the wall behind them.

He moved against her, the hard ridge of his arousal hitting her in just the right spot. She tightened her grip on him and moved with him, amping it up, pushing herself closer and closer to the edge.

He pressed a kiss to the center of her breasts, his tongue tracing a line down to the edge of the fabric of her dress. Then he continued down, still holding her leg as he lowered himself, draping her thigh over his shoulder as he settled onto his knees.

He pushed the skirt of her dress up, exposing her to him. "Remember, I told you I liked foreplay, but that first time...I took you too fast. I need to make up for it now."

"I... Oh." He slid his finger beneath her panties and stroked her where she was slick and so very ready for him.

She could feel his breath against her skin, hot and tantalizing. He ran his finger over her flesh, leaving a trail of fire in its wake. "Good, baby?" he asked.

"You told me not to talk," she said. "And now I can't. So don't ask questions. It's not fair."

"What's not fair is the fact that I'm shaking," he said, tugging her panties to the side, leaning in closer. "You do that to me, you know?"

She'd suddenly forgotten how to do anything but lean against that wall. "I didn't... I—"

Then his lips made contact with her bare skin and she couldn't think, couldn't breathe, and she definitely couldn't speak.

His tongue slid over her slick flesh, teasing her clitoris, sliding down deep inside of her. She flattened her hands against the wall, trying to find something to hold on to. Her fingers scraped against the stone, the rough surface biting her knuckles.

He moved his hand, his large palm cupping her butt, pulling her harder against his mouth as he intensified his attention on her body, his lips and tongue working dark magic on her, driving her closer and closer to the edge.

She put her hands on his shoulders, clinging to him, in an attempt to keep herself anchored to the earth.

He slid a finger deep inside of her and she tilted her head back, the stars in the darkening sky blurring, then he added a second and everything seemed to combust, the bright lights overhead bursting into a million fireworks.

He released her then stood, his body pressed against hers as he kissed her deeply, the evidence of her own desire on his lips. "Inside," he growled.

She turned away from him and fumbled for the door into the room. He slid it open and he walked in behind her, sweeping her hair over her shoulder, his lips on the back of her neck as they walked inside.

Then he gripped her shoulders and turned her to face him, kissing her lips. "Can't wait," he said, tugging at her dress until he slipped it from her body, then pulling her panties down her legs, while she worked on the closure to his jeans. He stripped them off, along with his underwear, leaving him blessedly naked.

He gripped her thighs and tugged her up so that her legs were wrapped around his waist before lowering them both to the carpet. The door was still open, the traffic noise and ocean breeze coming into the suite, but she didn't care.

There was nothing but this. Nothing but Alex.

"Please, Alex," she said. "I need you."

He positioned himself and slid inside of her, filling her, stretching her. She felt right for the first time in weeks. Or maybe more truthfully, she felt right for the first time in eleven years. More herself.

And then it was all wiped away as she gave up emotion for pleasure. There was nothing but their fractured breathing, Alex saying rough, coarse things in her ear. In English, in Greek. Words she'd never heard before. Words that sent a shiver of illicit longing through her, that heightened her desire, amped up her arousal.

After the orgasm he gave her outside, she was shocked that she had another one building already. But with each stroke, each rough, whispered word, he pushed her higher, faster.

He put his hand beneath her lower back, lifted her hips off of the ground and thrust harder into her, the sound of skin on skin overtaking the traffic noise from the street below.

He thrust into her one last time, a hoarse sound rising in his throat as he came. The sound, his loss of control, the look of tortured pleasure on his face, was so intense that she felt it as it echoed through her, grabbed hold of her own pleasure and expanded it, pushed her over the edge, their orgasms blending into one until she couldn't tell where hers began and ended, until she felt like they'd genuinely become one.

When it was over, the traffic noise came back into her consciousness. He rolled away from her, lying on his back on the carpet. A breeze blew through the door, chilling her bare, sweat-slicked skin.

"Well," she said.

"Yes." She looked over at him. He was on his back, his arms up, hands beneath his head.

"I suppose that was inevitable," she said, sitting up, drawing her knees to her chest.

"Clearly it was," he said.

"Obviously. Because it happened."

He turned and rose up, cupping her cheek. "Yes, it did."

"It didn't fix anything," she said, a cold feeling stealing into her chest.

"No, but I don't suppose sex ever stood a chance of fixing anything."

"I thought we might..." She stopped talking, because she didn't know what she'd thought. That it would steal the mystery? Break the bond? That it would bond them? Answer the questions and reservations she'd had?

No, she hadn't thought any of that. She'd thought of nothing but need. Her need to have him, the way he'd looked at her. The way he'd wanted her.

Not the façade, but her.

But now, with the haze of orgasm fading slowly into the

background, she was acutely aware of the fact that she was, yet again, naked with a man she didn't know. Yet again, she was exposed with him.

This time she'd gone and shown just how needy she was. For some kind of acceptance. It made her cringe. She knew better than to show this much of herself. Than to be anything more than self-contained.

Her mother had been that way. So perfect. So gracious. And she'd tried. Rachel had always tried, and never quite lived up to it all. She'd failed eleven years ago, on purpose and with blazing, spectacular glory because at the time it had seemed better than trying so hard and still not measuring up.

And she'd failed again with Alex.

"I think I need…"

"A cigarette?" he asked.

She laughed. "No. Oh, man…I haven't had a cigarette in…more than a decade."

"But you've had one? I'm shocked."

She took a deep breath. "I think you're too easily shocked. Everyone has a past, you know."

"Oh, believe me," he said. "I know about pasts."

"Yeah, I'm sure."

"You seem far too…good, to have a past," he said, frowning.

"I seem good? After that? I need to work on my moves."

"I just mean…you were a virgin. You've never had your name in the paper for anything even remotely scandalous."

"By design. All of it. Anyway, since when does virginity equal goodness? Mine's certainly not a reflection of that. It was…fear, mostly."

"You didn't seem afraid that night with me. Though you did tremble a bit."

"I hate you."

He stood up, naked still and entirely unconcerned.

"I'll bet the people in the building across the way are getting a show."

He turned and waved. "Probably."

"Good grief, Alex, have you no shame?"

"No. A product of my upbringing, I'm afraid. Hard to have shame raised in the environment I was."

"But the people across from us might have shame."

He grinned and bent, grabbing his black underwear and tugging them back on. "There, how's that?"

"Better for some," she said.

"Not you?"

She felt her face get hot. "Not really."

"How is it you kept all this passion hidden for so long?"

"I hid it so well, I even hid it from me," she said, hoping to redirect the subject. Away from things like this. Away from drunken parties and stupid decisions. "Plus… Look, I've made some crappy decisions, okay? And I almost got burned seriously and permanently because of it. Who am I kidding? I did get burned just…privately. I learned my lesson, though. I learned that you can't just do things without consequences catching up with you."

"Do you have lung problems from all your smoking?" he asked, his tone dry.

"If only that were the case."

They looked at each other for a second. She was still naked. And he was mostly naked. And she realized they knew so little about each other.

She knew about his past, but the only thing that felt real, the only thing that had seemed as if it was connected to a real emotion and not just a cold, hard fact about the way he'd grown up, was his honesty about the pizza.

They didn't know each other. He didn't know her. But then, as he'd already pointed out, no one really did.

And here she was, having just shared herself with him in the most intimate way, pregnant with his baby, no less, holding tight to shame that was so deeply embedded in her, trapped beneath that layer of steel.

"Do you know what I used to love?" she asked, because she was naked anyway, so there was no reason not to say it.

"What?" he asked.

"Driving really fast. I was…such a jerk behind the wheel. Really dangerous. Alana and I used to cruise around a lot when we were in Greece. We didn't really get the chance to drive in the city so when we were here…? All bets were off. I had this great car. It was red and sleek, and it went… well, it went fast, let's just say that. And we'd cruise with the top down and flirt with guys at stoplights. It made me feel like I wasn't Rachel Holt, this big disappointment to her mother. I hated all the things she wanted me to do. I just wanted to do something *I* wanted. And for a while, I just wanted to…forget that I cared and…drive fast."

"That's normal…isn't it? I don't really know since I didn't have what you'd call traditional teenage years, but even so, I think I've seen things like that in movies."

"Sure, I suppose it's normal. But that doesn't make it smart or safe. Especially not when you've been drinking. Which…we did. It was stupid. I was stupid and I…I don't know what I was doing. Rebelling against a life that was too…sedate, I suppose. A life I didn't feel like I was excelling at. I just wanted to feel something. Something exciting and dangerous. The wind in my hair, bubbles fizzing through my blood… I liked to flirt, too."

"You were an innocent, so it's not like—"

"There is a lot of ground between innocence and not having had intercourse, Alex. I would think a man like you would realize that," she said tightly.

"Oh." He looked…unhappy with that.

"Does that bother you? That you aren't the first man I've been intimate with? Though I'm not really sure you can call a quick blow job in the back of a car intimate. But

I make very poor decisions under the influence of drugs and alcohol, let's put it that way."

"This has never been in the papers. Everyone talks about you—"

"Like I'm the sainted Holt Heiress who spends her days sitting on a cloud playing a harp? I know. And it's not by accident. My father... He covered for me. He paid off every cop that pulled me over, he bought any incriminating club photos. He kept me from being exposed. And then..." Her throat tightened, a sick sense of shame pouring through her, choking her. "I did something...really stupid. That seems to be the only descriptor I have for that year of my life. One year, Alex. Out of...twenty-eight. I acted out and I almost lost everything. I almost changed the way people saw me forever. I...I know I did change the way my mother and father saw me."

"What happened?" he asked, his posture suddenly stiff, something in his stance deceptively, unnaturally still. As though energy were building in him, coiling tightly beneath the surface of his skin, ready to pounce at any moment on an imagined enemy.

Too bad the only enemy was her. The things, the desires, in her.

"Everything kind of came to a head—bad choice of words, you'll see why in a second—when I met this guy at a club. Colin. I really liked him. We met up and danced a couple of weekends in a row and he asked if I wanted to 'get out of here,' which, you know, means that a guy wants something from you. I was drunk and feeling like giving it because he was hot and I liked him. A lot. He was handsome, and he had a nice smile. He thought I was pretty." She rolled her eyes then looked down at her hands. She didn't want to look at Alex right now.

This reminded her of standing in her father's office, sweating and shaking, about to embarrass herself fatally, because she didn't know what else to do. Because if she didn't expose herself to her father, she would be exposing herself to the whole world.

"Anyway, I ended up in the backseat of the car with him. Which... You know what that means. We parked at the beach. At least it wasn't a back parking lot somewhere— that makes it less sordid. Kind of. He got out his video camera. Pre the days of cell phone recordings, and thank God because the whole thing was much more concrete back then, not this nebulous digital web that could have had it in a thousand places immediately."

"What did he do?"

"He filmed me. He asked and I thought, why not? I thought it was hot that he wanted to commemorate the event. I was drunk. I was seventeen. And right when he asked me to do it I thought maybe I even loved him, because being drunk and seventeen is basically all it takes to feel like you love someone. He wanted me, and I... Well, what I really loved was being wanted. For me, you know. Because, clearly, my blow job skills were the essence of me as a woman."

"He videotaped you..."

"Going down on him. Yes. And the next morning I woke up with a raging headache and very little memory of it. Until he came around the villa the following evening looking for things to go further. I said no because...I didn't feel ready for sex yet. Which maybe doesn't make a lot of sense but...I just knew I wasn't. He got mad and he threatened me. Because he had the video and he was going to send it out. To the media, to the internet. And I was...so afraid that he would. That...*that* would be out there. Me...doing that. Thinking about it makes me panic even now. I just...can't imagine anything more exposing or humiliating. Though telling my father about it and begging him to bail me out was a close second."

"And what happened?"

"He made it all go away. He protected me, because that's what he's always done. But he…he was so disappointed, I could tell. And that was when he told me he wasn't protecting me anymore. He told me that anything could have happened to me. Driving drunk, going off with strange men… He said I was going to get myself killed and he wouldn't watch while I did it. He wouldn't enable it. No more help. No more money. No more family. He said I had to behave myself, or lose everything. And…I have. Until now. Probably I'm cut off, I suppose, but…but…"

"That's why you aren't calling home."

She nodded silently. "I don't want to know." Her eyes stung, but still, there were no tears. "I don't want to see him look at me that way ever again. Like I'm a…lost cause. I don't know why I did all that stuff, not really. But I know why I stopped. Because I wanted more out of my life than what I was going to get partying until my brain fell out of my ear."

"And that more was marrying a man you didn't love or even want to sleep with?"

His words hit her, cold and hard in the chest.

"Apparently, what I was really waiting for was to meet a stranger and have a one-night stand with him and get pregnant with his baby. My goals were much loftier than a mere loveless marriage."

He cleared his throat and looked out the window. "Did your father tell you what a worthless asshole that man was?"

"What?"

"Did he tell you what a horrible person that man was? Because it seems to me that all of this was about the situation you put yourself in, and while I get that there were poor decisions on your part—and I'm the proud owner of many poor decisions so I'm not throwing stones—he was the one determined to take a private encounter public. He was the one who was threatening to expose you."

"I... He wasn't there to be lectured, I was."

"And you were the one who had to change."

"I really did though, Alex. I was trying to take a long walk off a short pier."

"I agree with that in terms of the substance abuse. Drugs mess things up, Rachel, in ways I'm sure you never saw in a club. But you're clean now, I assume."

She nodded. "Yes. I was never a heavy user. Mainly I drank too much alcohol. But I have a one-glass limit on wine now. And a no-glass limit at the moment."

"What were you trying to fix?"

"What?" she asked.

"Everyone I've ever known that's been on drugs or who partied till they couldn't think—and I've known a lot of them, considering my background—has been running from something. Medicating for some reason. What was yours?"

"I don't... I..." She blinked rapidly and looked away from him. "I didn't worry so much about being good enough when I was doing all that. I felt...happy. I felt good."

"And since you stopped?"

She lifted one shoulder. "Until recently, I knew I was good. Feelings didn't really matter."

"So you exchanged one form of denying your feelings for another? New solution—don't change your feelings, just don't have them?"

"I'm sorry, Alex, but this is something you couldn't possibly know anything about."

"Is that right?"

"Yes. I don't mean to be cruel, but who has any expectation of you? When I found out who you were I knew I'd been used because your name is synonymous with epic bastardry. You'd already tried to ruin Ajax with those tax fraud allegations."

He quirked his lips into a half smile. "And the odds that they were true seemed high. They would have been with many corporations."

"Sadly for you, Ajax does things so by the book it's almost unreal."

"A surprise, considering."

She suddenly felt even more naked than she had a moment ago. She wrapped her arms around herself and shivered. She should get her clothes, but she had a feeling that they wouldn't make her any warmer. Any less exposed. He knew now. He knew the worst of her.

And she knew...what he thought was the worst of Ajax. And she knew about the pizza. But she didn't know him.

"Tell me something about you," she said. "What are you ashamed of?"

He looked away from her. "I'm not ashamed of anything. I don't have shame."

He looked back at her, their eyes meeting, his expression fierce. "I've seen too many things...done too many things. And I don't regret them. Because they've made me who I am."

"That's such a line. We all regret things. I regret getting into the car with Colin. I regret drinking that much. I regret letting him videotape me."

"And it changes nothing, so why bother with it?"

"Because it did change something. It changed me."

"Ah, yes, and you're so happy and well-adjusted now?"

"No. I've proven, yet again, that when you follow your... emotions and hormones and...things that aren't logical, stupid things happen."

"Is that how you see the baby? As something stupid?"

"I didn't say that."

"You said stupid things happen."

"Are we going to stand here and pretend I made a stellar

decision in sleeping with you when I was engaged to someone else? I don't have it in me to lie like that."

"Just to omit the truth when it suits you."

"Shut up, Alex."

"You just asked me to share about myself."

"Then do that. But don't throw stones at me. I can't take it right now. I just…spilled my guts to you and I can't take your criticism on top of it."

Silence fell between them. A thick blanket that offered no warmth or comfort. Just a heavy awkwardness that made her skin break out into goose bumps.

He shook his head. "Sorry, I'm not overly shocked by your revelations since I used to catch live performances of what you did in that video in the halls of…of the Kouklakis compound. When I was a child," he finished, the word hard and bitter. "I was protected, but only to a degree. You want me to tell you about things I'm ashamed of? I don't even know what shame looks like."

He turned away from her, his posture rigid, the defined muscles in his back standing out, tension radiating from him. "I've seen my own mother on her knees in front of a man. I've seen her beg and cry and offer favors for a chance to stay." He turned back to her. "To take care of me, I thought. Because of love, I thought. But that wasn't it. At least it wasn't because she loved me. It was because she loved heroin and the man who owned it all. It was never for me. Fine, do you want to know what shame really feels like? Finding out your own mother loves drugs and sex more than she loves you. That's shame. That burns, Rachel, in a way you can't possibly imagine. You want to know what I know about family? There you are."

"Alex…"

"Don't," he bit out, crossing to her. "I don't need your pity. I am not that boy. I am not a victim. I got out by the skin of my teeth—I scraped my knuckles raw climbing out of that prison. I didn't escape clean, but I escaped."

"Is that why you hate Ajax so much? Because he got out and he's done well for himself? Because he's unaffected?"

"Of course that's part of why I hate him."

Because Ajax was so normal. And Alex was so broken. He didn't say the words but she felt them between them. And she believed him.

"What happened when you left?"

He reached out, cupping the back of her head and pulling her forward. "I do not want to talk anymore."

"Alex—"

He kissed her, his lips hard, crushing against hers.

"Don't be afraid with me, Rachel," he said, his hands skimming over her curves. "Don't hide from me."

"Alex," she said again, his name a plea this time. For what, she wasn't sure. For freedom? For a moment unleashed from the cage she'd locked herself in.

"There's no shame with me," he said against her lips. "None at all."

His words pulled at something inside of her, at a need she'd been denying for so long. Rooted out the guilt that had been tangled around her soul like a creeping vine.

"You want me," he said, kissing her neck, her collarbone. "Tell me that you want me."

"I can't…"

"Tell me what you want," he said, his voice firm as he lowered his head and sucked her nipple deep into his mouth.

"We just did this, like, a half an hour ago," she said, gasping, her head falling back.

"Yes. I know. And you want me again already. Because you're passionate, Rachel, no matter what you think. Because you have desire. So much. And it's beautiful."

Her throat closed, something shifting in her chest. She took a sharp breath, trying to hold back the sudden, unexpected rush of emotion. She didn't have time for it. Not now. Not when Alex was kissing her like this. Not when he was taking that old memory she'd just shared and twisting it, changing the way she felt about it. Changing the way she felt about herself.

"Tell me what you want," he growled.

"You," she said.

"Tell me how I make you feel," he said, raising his head, his teeth scraping against her neck before he sucked the gentle curve hard, drawing away the sting.

"I…I want you, Alex."

"Like no one else?"

"No one else."

He put his hand between her thighs, his thumb sliding over her clitoris while he pushed a finger deep inside of her. "Tell me," he said again, a ragged edge to his voice that told her there would be no arguing with him. That told her she had to obey.

"I—" The words stuck in her throat, embarrassment, and self-protection slamming down and keeping her from saying anything.

"Tell me," he said, "or you don't get to come."

"Alex," she said, trying to be exasperated while his hands were working magic on her body. While he was holding her apart from paradise.

"I don't have time for you to hide, *agape.* You want me, or you don't. But you have to tell me." He added a second finger, amped up the movements, pushing her closer but still not taking her there. And he knew it.

"I…I want you inside of me."

He smiled, wicked, naughty. Thrilling. "I am inside of you."

She shook her head. "That's not what I mean."

"Say what you mean."

"I don't…"

"You want my cock?" She nodded, biting her lip hard. "Then tell me."

Heat flooded her face—embarrassment and arousal. So silly when she was being so intimate with him. When they'd done even more only a half hour ago, why couldn't she say what she wanted? Why was it so hard to be honest? With him? With herself?

"I want your cock inside of me," she said, the words coming out in a rush.

He cupped her chin, held her face steady while he kissed her deep. He withdrew his fingers from her and lifted her up into his arms, carrying her into the bedroom and depositing her on the center of the bed, pushing his underwear down his legs and coming to join her.

He parted her thighs and gripped his thick erection, pressing himself to the entrance of her body, guiding himself in slowly.

She arched, a harsh cry escaping her lips as he filled her. Stretched her. She felt so close, so needy—incredibly, considering what had happened earlier. But she couldn't get enough of him.

She'd been waiting for this, for him, all of her life.

As soon as she had the thought, she pushed it away. She pushed everything away. The barrier she kept between herself and the world.

She forgot to feel shame. She forgot to curb her emotions. She forgot to be quiet and dignified. Instead she clung to his shoulders, dug her nails into his skin and wrapped her legs around his hips.

Instead she bit his neck and cried out her pleasure, riding the wave of pleasure to ecstasy. He pounded hard into her body until he stiffened, a hoarse cry on his lips as he found his own pleasure, as he poured himself into her.

Afterward she lay there, shaking. Feeling vulnerable and

exposed. Like a creature that had been dragged out of its den and forced into the sunlight, uncovered, unprotected.

And she started retreating as quickly as possible. Did her best to try and rebuild her defense system.

But his arms were around her and he was kissing her neck, her shoulder, the curve of her breast. It made it impossible to retreat fully. Because he was holding her captive.

"You can't possibly want to do that again," she said. "I'm completely spent."

"That's one of the perks of younger men," he said, pinching her nipple lightly. "We can go all night."

"I can't. I'm exhausted." Physically, she could have him again. She already wanted him. How could she ever get tired of a man like him?

But emotionally? She didn't have the strength. Because he'd done something to her. It was more than unleashing a wild part of herself she hadn't known existed. It was more than just sex. She was stripped naked, down to her soul, and there was no way she could go through any more just yet.

It was all starting to catch up with her. The reality of her actions, from the moment she'd met him until she'd told him so bluntly what she'd wanted from him.

She looked at him, their eyes clashing. He was so beautiful. A man built to tempt even the most righteous of women. And she'd never been all that righteous. She'd only been pretending.

This man was the father of her baby.

Her stomach lurched, the thought butting up hard against her compromised defenses. Oh, good Lord, the baby...

She shivered, a dry sob in her throat. But still there were no tears.

"What's wrong?" he asked.

"I don't know...I...I was thinking about the baby."

He froze behind her, then his hand drifted from her breast down to her stomach. "How are you feeling about it?"

Scared. "Okay. I mean…it's a lot to deal with."

"Naturally. And what are your plans?" he asked. "If you don't marry me, what do you think we'll do?"

"I don't want to talk about this right now." She felt scrubbed raw, and she didn't think she could even handle thinking about the pregnancy in terms of it producing an actual baby at the end, much less how Alex and her relationship with him would squeeze in around that.

"Then when, Rachel? You're pregnant with my child. You continue to end up in my bed. Marriage is—"

"Is that what this is about?"

"What?"

"You…putting the moves on me. Is it just so I'll agree to this…marriage thing?"

"This marriage thing," he said, moving away from her and getting off of the bed, "is the best chance our child has at a normal life."

"Oh! So we're normal? What in all the world makes you think that?"

"I didn't say we were, but a normal family structure is the best chance this child has."

"And you want to prove something to Ajax?"

"This has nothing to do with Ajax! When I went to that wedding, I went for you. You could have been marrying my very best friend and I would have come to take you. Because you're mine. It's that simple."

"I'm yours? Why?"

"Because," he said, his words tight. "Because you're having my baby."

"You didn't know I was."

"And because I want you."

"To be who you want. To do what you want."

His lips curled. "I asked what you wanted. And you told me. Oh, baby, did you tell me."

"Shut up, Alex," she said, turning away from him, those words starting to become familiar.

"Because you still want to pretend that you're a cyborg?"

"Because I can't deal with all of this right now!" she said, exploding. "With the baby. And with you…and…and my family… I can't." She got out of bed and started hunting for her clothes.

"We have to deal with it sometime."

She had that feeling again. As if the pressure was too much. As if she was too full of…everything and as if there was no release on the horizon. As if she was drowning inside of herself.

"Not right now," she said. She looked around and realized her clothes were in the living room. "Crap."

She pulled the blankets off the bed and gathered them around her body, covering up her curves. "I'm going to bed," she said.

"Fine."

"And I'm not marrying you."

"Yet," he said, his blue eyes boring into hers. Oh, those eyes…

"Why does it matter to you? You don't know anything about normal. You said yourself your experience with family is…is horrible, so why would you care?"

"Because I will give better than that for my child. I can't fix anything that happened to me. I can't…make it go away. But I can make sure no son or daughter of mine is exposed to what I was. That they'll always know who their mother and father are. That we'll both be there for them. If that's not what you want…perhaps you should give custody of the child to me."

Her entire body recoiled at the thought. "No. I would never give up my baby."

"You said yourself you aren't sure how you feel about it."

"Because I'm afraid. Because I know what a huge responsibility it is! Because I don't want to...raise a child who grows up like me and I don't know how not to do that. How to protect a child without smothering them. How to guide them without making them feel like their choices are all bad....how to protect them when they genuinely are being an idiot. I don't even know who I am, Alex. How am I supposed to deal with the life of another human being?"

"With me," he said, his voice rough.

"No offense, but I'm not sure adding screwed up to screwed up is going to equal anything more than a mess."

She turned and walked out of the room, her chest swollen, her body aching.

She didn't know how to fix this. She didn't know what she wanted. Right now she could hardly remember how to breathe.

CHAPTER NINE

IT HAD BEEN TWO WEEKS since Cannes. And two weeks since they'd last had sex. And Alex was pretty sure his head was going to explode, if parts farther south didn't first.

He had no idea how to reach her. He'd never wanted to reach a woman before, not in any way beyond the physical. But Rachel... He wanted something more from her. Without having to give more than was comfortable. Surely that wasn't completely unreasonable.

She didn't want all he had to give anyway.

Not if she had any concept of what it might mean.

Hell, he wasn't sure he had a complete concept of what it might mean and he didn't aim to acquire one.

Still, she was staying with him, even if she was wandering around sniffing indignantly at him half of the time. She was hiding, and he knew it. But he found he didn't care, so long as she was close. Barring the small blip of a headline about them cavorting in paradise, which had something to do with them being snapped together having dinner in Cannes, no one had picked up on what was actually happening, and considering the tenuous situation, that was fine with him.

She seemed pale, though. More so than when they'd first met, and he hated the idea that he might be the cause of it. Shouldn't be surprised, though. That came back to him.

To what was in him. A boy that no one could love, a man who was fundamentally flawed down to his very genetics.

That black blood filtering through his veins. The image he could never quite shake.

He saw her sitting out on the terrace and walked through the room, out the door, to join her. "Good morning," he said.

"Hi."

"Ready for the doctor to come?"

"Yes. It seems pretty extravagant to have her do a house call."

"Until you're ready for the story to break, we need to keep it as low key and close to home as possible. I assume you aren't ready?"

"No. I haven't told my father yet."

"Have you spoken to him?"

She nodded. "Very briefly. He's worried. I told him… I told him that I was just enjoying a little bit of fun. He said…" She blinked rapidly. "He said that was fine. That it was about time I did. Why is he so supportive of me? Even when I make such stupid mistakes?"

"Why shouldn't he be?"

"I don't know. I guess it would make more sense if he'd just get mad."

"Why? You're a grown woman. You can make your own decisions."

"I'm not sure if I make good ones."

A maid appeared in the doorway. "Dr. Sands is here."

"Great. Send her in," Alex said.

Dr. Sands, Rachel's doctor, whom he hadn't met yet, came out onto the terrace smiling. It felt so strange to have a doctor standing there. To know that this was about the baby.

Sometimes—well, all the time—it was so much easier not to think about the baby.

But then, if there was no baby, Rachel would have no reason to be there.

That made his throat tighten with a strange kind of terror.

"Hi, Rachel. Shall we go upstairs and get started?"

Rachel looked at him, her eyes wide.

"Are you afraid I'll come?" he asked. "Or afraid I won't?"

She lifted a shoulder. "I'm not sure."

"I'm going to come."

"Okay."

A loose summer dress and a sheet were Rachel's accessories for the appointment. She knew it was technically too early to need another appointment. She was close to eight weeks, but there was little point in checking things out. Except she was nervous.

About everything. Afraid everything was fine. Afraid it wasn't.

And on the verge of losing her mind completely. The pressure in her chest had built to a maddening degree. So that just breathing every day was a chore.

It had been two weeks since she'd been with Alex. Two weeks. And she'd denied herself the only release that had given her any relief. Because he was too much. Because he wanted too much.

"Go ahead and lie down on the bed, Rachel, it will be pretty quick. I understand that you were wanting to see if we could see the heartbeat. I can't make any guarantees. If we don't see anything, it could all still be fine, but we'll give it a look."

She nodded. "Thank you. I know it's early but...we have...things to deal with."

Dr. Sands gave her a sympathetic smile. "I know. It's okay, we'll figure it all out."

"Alex, could you stand up...well, not down there?" Rachel asked as she moved into position for her exam.

Alex came to stand by her head as the doctor prepared the ultrasound.

Rachel winced both at the cold and the intrusion and waited for everything to come up on the small screen of the portable machine.

"There we go," Dr. Sands said. "See the flutter of movement there? That's the heartbeat."

Rachel looked at the black space on the screen, at the little lines of white and flickering brightness that signified life.

"It all looks good. Of course, there are no guarantees at any stage," she said, looking her in the eyes, "so you don't want to make any decisions that are too life-changing. But you're healthy, and there's no reason to believe anything will go wrong, okay?"

Rachel nodded. "Okay. That's great. Good."

"I'll let you get cleaned up. Alex? Perhaps you'd like to come with me. And if you have any questions it would be a good time—"

Their voices faded when the door closed and Rachel stood up, her hands shaking as she went into the bathroom and dealt with the gel mess left behind by the ultrasound.

Then she knelt down in front of the toilet and threw up.

Morning sickness in the afternoon maybe. Or just shock.

She sat down in the middle of the floor, her knees drawn up to her chest. What had she gotten herself into? She was pregnant and there was really no denying it. There was a heartbeat. Inside of her. She'd never been so afraid in her entire life.

She didn't know how to do this. She didn't know… She couldn't do it.

All she could picture now was the doctor putting the baby in her arms and her handing it right back.

She pushed herself up, standing on shaking legs. She felt like a newborn fawn. A newborn fawn that was in no way equipped to care for a baby because she was...well, she didn't feel like she was a grown-up yet. Didn't feel like she could be a mom.

Miserable, she crossed to the sink and started brushing her teeth. At least her breath would be better, even if everything in her was still in disarray.

She took a deep breath, gasped for it, and went back into the bedroom. She was okay. She would be okay. She didn't need to cry.

She never cried. She hadn't cried in years. She wasn't about to start now. She hadn't cried since her mother had died. Her mother...

That's not where it goes, Rachel.

No, Rachel, you're doing it wrong.

You're too loud. Too rowdy. You shouldn't go out at night. You shouldn't wear that dress.

Rachel, how could you do something like that? Didn't I teach you to wait for your husband?

Rachel blinked rapidly, trying to shut out the memories. The critical voice in her head. The voice of the woman who was perfect and graceful to everyone. Everyone but her.

Because Rachel couldn't do anything right. Rachel wasn't ever going to be able to do things the way they were supposed to be done. Rachel would never get it right. Ever.

She'd tried to kick against it, to rebel, and in the end she was the only one who'd been hurt. And she'd come out the other side trying so hard to be better. Trying to keep herself from being too big...too loud...too *her*.

She was trying so hard not to be herself.

The dam that was holding everything in, that had been holding it all in for years in spite of the mounting pressure, finally burst.

A tear slid down her cheek.

The first tear in years. And now she didn't think they would ever stop.

She walked over to the bed, clutching her chest, her shoulders shaking as the dam burst on the past ten years of emotion, held so tightly in her, in a tight, heavy ball that she'd resigned herself to carrying around inside forever, broke open and poured out all over the place.

She wondered if you could drown in your own tears. She was seriously afraid she might. Or at least that she might die from not being able to catch her breath. Every attempt at breathing became another sob, until she was gasping, shaking and having a complete and utter breakdown.

Maybe this was what happened when you kept it all in. Maybe the breaking point was inevitable.

She was certainly broken. No question.

She was dimly aware of the bedroom door opening.

"Rachel?" Alex's voice, her name followed by a sharp curse. "What's wrong? Is everything okay? Are you okay?"

"I can't do this, Alex!" Her words came from somewhere deep inside of her, came out without her having a chance to even think them first. She only felt them.

"Yes, you can."

"No, I can't. I can't…ever do things the way they're supposed to be done. I mess them up. When I feel too much I make mistakes and when I…when I don't feel at all I feel like I might as well be doing nothing at all. I don't know what I'm supposed to do. I don't know how to love a child, and follow my heart, use my emotions, without making bad decisions. And if I…if I keep on like I have been and just don't care…then what's the point? I can't. It's too hard. I'll mess it all up, I know I will."

His arms were around her, holding her close, his lips on her temple, fingers laced through her hair. Their last confrontation, the angry words, didn't evaporate, but for the moment they were on hold. "Rachel, you can do this. You can."

"It's a lie, Alex. It's always been a lie. I'm not perfect. I hide all these pieces of myself, and I don't show anyone. I don't know how to give everything because I'm so damn afraid of it. Because if I do…it still won't be good enough. It won't ever be good enough."

"Why do you think that?"

"Because it never was! Not ever. Not for her. I tried, Alex, I put everything on hold because she was sick. I helped plan her parties, I chose Ajax because he was safe and easy and he wouldn't disgrace me or our family. I tried to appear polished and to always smile, just like she did. But all I could ever be was a pale imitation. All I could ever manage was lukewarm cocktail shrimp and a party that was barely mediocre. She was this… She made everyone so happy at parties. She made everyone's life easier and I just…made things harder because I was distracted and couldn't finish, or just because I don't have that thing that she had. I fake it, but I don't have it. Not really. The press sees it, they think I'm so like her but I… She was never happy."

"That isn't your fault, Rachel, you aren't her clone. It doesn't mean you're a failure, not in any way."

She nodded. "I'm just all…messed up inside, Alex."

He stroked her hair, his body a solid wall of reassurance for her to lean against. "Aren't we all?"

"Well, *we* are."

"As you said. Screwed up and screwed up."

"A mess," she said.

"But it's the mess we have."

"I know," she said, sniffing loudly. "I haven't even cried for… This is the first time in eight years."

"I haven't cried since I was a boy," he said.

"How long?" she wanted to know. She wanted to know how heavy the burden inside of him was. Hers had been nearly unbearable.

"Probably about twelve years. A boy of fourteen—I might have cried then."

"Why?"

"You want my secrets now, *agape?*"

"I'm leaving snot trails all over your shirt," she said, leaning back. "I think we have no reason to keep secrets. And I wanted them once already. But you didn't give them."

She thought back to their night in Cannes. He'd deflected then. Both times. And he'd done it with sex.

"Then you can have them now," he said. "Leaving the Kouklakis compound was the single hardest thing I ever did. The worst day of my life. My mother was dead. I felt very alone. Afraid of what was ahead. I wanted to escape and yet I feared the freedom. I knew I couldn't stay be-cause…because of what I would become if I did. I cried that day. It was the only home I knew, and I loved it as much as I hated it."

"Your problems are so much bigger than mine," she said. "I must seem like a nutcase to you."

"No. I don't see it that way."

"How?"

"Because it hurts you. If there's one thing I've learned from being in the position I've been in, being around the types of people I've been exposed to, it's that people have common pains. They come from different places, but they are the same sorts of hurts."

"Forgive me, Alex, but you're one of the most amoral men I've ever met. You used me to get back at Ajax, you were going to crash my wedding—"

"Maybe. I was undecided. Though…it is likely I would have stopped you from going through with it. Because… as I said, you are mine."

"You…don't make any sense to me," she said. "You act like you were raised by wolves…and then you go and say things like this. You go and say things that are so insightful, and that make me feel like I just might not be alone, or that I might not be the big ball of crazy I tend to think I am."

"You probably are still a...ball of crazy," he said, the words sounding so funny and off rhythm in that accent. "But a very charming one."

"Thanks. I appreciate that."

"Well, I can't have you questioning what you think of me too deeply. It might make you rethink too many things, right?"

"Maybe I should." She rose up onto her knees and moved to where he stood at the edge of the bed. Her heart was pounding fast, the emotion flowing through her making her dizzy.

She knew she shouldn't touch him. She knew she shouldn't want him. Nothing was settled. There was still too much baggage between them. But when she was in Alex's arms...she was so much closer to the woman she really was, rather than the woman who was just pretending.

Right now, she didn't have the strength to pretend. She leaned in, eye level with his chest, and kissed the bare skin revealed by his undone top button.

"Rachel." Her gaze met his. He looked like he was in pain, his eyes closed, a deep groove between his brows.

"I'm not going to hit you," she said, stretching up higher and kissing his neck, "I just want to kiss you."

He reached out and grabbed her wrist, held her back from him, his eyes. "Only if you're absolutely certain you want me to push you back onto that bed and take you hard and fast. Make you mine. Make you scream."

"I think I do," she said, her voice trembling, her whole body trembling.

He captured her face with his other hand, his expression intense. "That isn't good enough. You'd better be completely certain."

She swallowed hard. "I want you, Alex."

"Why?" he asked, his voice sharp.

"I don't know why," she said, a tear sliding down her face. Another tear, nothing significant about this one, since it was the hundred-somethingth tear in an hour instead of the first one in eight years. But still, it felt significant. Everything about this moment did.

"Try to tell me."

"Because you're the only man that's ever made me feel this way. Because you're the only man I've ever wanted, *really* wanted. You make me feel like myself. And I don't think I've ever felt like just...me, before. Everything I've done, from rebellion to behaving, has been for other people. You were the first thing I ever did for me."

"I see." He traced her jawline with his fingertip. "Am I still a mistake to you, Rachel?"

"I don't know yet."

"What? You need to...make me one more time before you're sure?"

"I might need to get to the end of...everything before I know for sure."

"And in the meantime you want to make love with me?"

She nodded slowly, his hands still holding her. "Yes. Does that make me... Is there something wrong with me?"

"There's something wrong with both of us. Because whether I should or not, I'm going to have you tonight."

"When you say things like that... Alex, it's enough to drive a woman totally insane. And in a good way."

"Is it?"

"No one else has ever wanted me. Not really. Not me."

"I do," he said. "Feel how much?" He put her hand on his chest, over his heart, then guided it downward, over his denim-covered erection. "Do you feel that?"

"Yes," she said, squeezing him. "Impossible not to."

"Then you can't be in any doubt of how much I want

you. Want this. If you're sure of one thing, be sure of me. Of how much I want you."

"You really do say nice things."

"I'm honest. When I want to be."

"That instills a lot of confidence," she said, moving her hand over him, cupping him through his jeans. "I think you should take these off."

"In a moment. I want to watch you take your dress off. We're always in a hurry. I don't want to rush this."

"I might not give you a choice," she said, moving away from him to the center of the bed and sliding a strap from her shoulder. "I might jump on you."

"I welcome the challenge," he said. "You wouldn't be half so much fun if you weren't always pushing me."

"You actually enjoy my back talk?" she asked, pushing down the second strap.

"I more than enjoy it. It turns me on. I've seen enough passive, hollow-eyed women, bent on doing what they're told just to get a fix. Of a drug. Of a person. I don't want that from you. I don't want empty compliance or…that thing that you've been doing where you try to make everyone's life easy at the expense of what you want. I want fire."

She smiled and tugged at the zipper on the back of her dress, letting it fall down, revealing her breasts. "I think I can give you that."

She was trying to keep it light, keep it sassy, but it was hard to do when she felt as if she might cave in on herself. As if all the emotion that was inside of her was going to expand too far, and when everything came to a crashing halt, she would just fold right in.

She pushed the dress over her hips. The sunlight was bright, filtering in through the window, and she was naked now. But she didn't feel awkward. She felt incredible. Because he did want her. Because he didn't want her as the woman she was when she put on her mask and tried to become the perfect hostess. The one who never sent a ripple over the surface of anyone's life.

He was okay with her not falling in line. With her not being perfect.

"I'll never be perfect," she said, the words spilling out of her mouth. She was physically naked, so she might as well be emotionally naked, too.

"I don't know what you're talking about. You look completely perfect to me."

"You're just saying that because I'm naked," she said. "But that's not what I mean. I mean...I'm never going to be everything that my mother was. I try. But I can't sing on key. And I don't like big fancy parties that much. I like to stay home in my pajamas instead of going to galas. I hate those stupid art shows that she used to sponsor. Generalizing, but I kinda think that modern art is pretentious and I never want to have to go host anything like that ever again."

"Then why do you?"

"Because I don't know how else to be...valuable."

"Right now, touching you seems like it's more important than air. I feel like if I don't touch you, if I don't have you, I might die. How's that?"

"That feels good. Not an overarching life goal, but good enough for now."

He put one knee on the edge of the bed and tugged her toward him, kissing her deeply, his arm tight around her waist, hand resting on the curve of her butt as he explored her slowly with his lips and tongue.

"You are," he said, pausing to kiss her again, "the most incredible woman. The most beautiful. The most frustrating. You are, I hate to say, a terrible singer. But how could you ever doubt your value?"

He kissed her neck and she shivered, whatever words she was going to say drying up on her tongue, stolen completely by his touch, by her desire for him.

Alex advanced on her, strong arms guiding her fall to the soft mattress as he came to rest over her, one of his hands pinning both of hers above her head.

"You've said that I made you do things that weren't in your character," he said, "but you have turned me into a man I barely know. I dream of you. Of the softness of your skin. The sounds you make when you come. I think about you the way you told me what you wanted from me." Her face heated at the memory. "You are a distraction," he said. "One I never expected to deal with. I can't even think of revenge, and *agape,* I was able to think of revenge when I was starving on the streets, when I made my first million, my first billion. I have always been able to think of it. And for the first time my head is so full of other things, other desires, that I can't. That is what you do to me. That is powerful. You have done more than make me act out of character—you've changed me."

She wiggled, wanting to touch his face.

'No," he said, tracing her nipple with his free hand. "I'm not letting you free just yet."

"Why?" she asked, panting, out of breath, needing him so badly she thought she might go crazy.

"Because I want to take my time." He lowered his head, sucking her nipple deep into his mouth. "I want to savor you."

He lifted his hand to cup her cheek and she nipped at his finger. He paused, a smile curving his lips, his finger hovering just above her mouth. She sucked it in deep, the expression on his face taking on that slightly pained look, then as she released him, she bit him gently.

"You are dangerous," he said. He bent and kissed her, bit her bottom lip as they separated. "But so am I."

"I never doubted you were dangerous," she said, trying to catch her breath. "But I'm not."

"You don't think?"

"No."

"Liar. You are completely deadly. To my sanity. To my senses. I don't even think I can breathe right when I look at you."

His free hand roamed over her curves while he held her still. She arched and squirmed, trying to find satisfaction. Trying to find release. But he held her, held the power to bring her to orgasm or not. And he was definitely enjoying teasing her at the moment.

"Please, Alex."

"Please what?" he asked, kissing her neck, the curve of her breast. He settled between her thighs, the denim rough on her skin. And she moved against him, desperate for satisfaction.

"Please let me…"

"Please let you…? Remember, you have to ask. Don't hide from me, Rachel. Tell me what you want."

"Please let me come," she said, her cheeks getting hot with arousal, not embarrassment.

"Good things come to those who wait," he said.

"I've been waiting. I've been waiting for two weeks."

"So have I," he said. "And I want to enjoy the experience."

He moved away from her on the bed and tugged his shirt over his head. She watched the play of his muscles rippling beneath golden skin as he worked on his belt and shrugged his pants and underwear down his legs.

"I want you," she said.

"I know."

"I mean…get off the bed."

"I don't take orders."

"You should take these. Now get off the bed."

He obeyed, standing close, and she moved over to the edge, on her knees. "I want this." She lowered her head, her heart hammering hard. And she realized she really did want this. She wanted to taste him. Not because it would pleasure him, but because she wanted it. Wanted him in her mouth. Her tongue flicking out to taste the head of his shaft.

Strong fingers gripped her hair, gently pulling her back. "You don't have to do that."

"I know." She met his eyes. "I want to, Alex."

His hold on her loosened and she bent down again, taking him into her mouth. The sharp hiss of his breath, the tenseness in his whole body, sent a sharp pang of pleasure straight to her stomach.

She was so very aware that this was Alex. The past wasn't with them. There was nothing shameful tied to what she was doing for him, because she wanted it. Because it wasn't selfish taking and coercion on his end.

"Stop, Rachel."

"Why?"

"We're savoring, remember?"

"I know I am," she said.

He growled and she found herself flat on her back. He had one arm wrapped around her, the other cupping her chin. "You push me to the edge of my control."

His kiss was hard, demanding, his tongue sliding over hers, the slick friction sending a wave of lust through her body.

"I'd hate to see you out of control then," she said, panting as they parted. "I'm not sure I could take it."

He chuckled, the sound void of warmth. "Perhaps not." He tightened his hold on her and repositioned them so that they were on their sides with him behind her. "Then again...I might be able to do good things with my loss of control."

He cupped her breast with one hand, turned her face toward him with the other and kissed her lips. She could feel his erection, hard and hot against her back.

He took his hand from her breast and positioned himself at the entrance to her body, testing her before sliding in deep. She let her head fall back against him, tasting him as deeply as she could in her current position.

His hand drifted between her thighs, stroking her clit as he thrust inside of her. He held her to him, his arm tight over her chest, his breath hot on her neck as he whispered dark, sensual words in her ear.

Alex liked to talk dirty. And he did it so well. Telling her how good she felt and all the things he wanted to do with her, in explicit detail.

She was hot all over, pleasure coiling low and tight inside of her, breathing a near impossibility.

"Come for me," he said. "You wanted to. Now you have my permission."

It shouldn't have been sexy. But the words, low and husky and so commanding, pushed her over the edge. A hoarse cry escaped her lips as he thrust into her one last time, pleasure pounding through her like a wave, enhanced by the pulse of his shaft as he found his own release.

She lay back against him, breathing hard, her body tingling with pleasure, her lungs burning. Her heart was pounding hard, and it hurt. Because it felt heavy, swollen. She couldn't begin to put a name to what it was, only that it made her feel happy and desperately sad at the same time.

She wanted him. In every way. Wanted to have this, to keep him with her. And she knew that it wasn't going to happen. She'd refused him. And he was young. He would meet someone new. He would make a family with her. He would do this with her.

And she could only think of one thing to say.

"I'll marry you, Alex."

CHAPTER TEN

ALEX WAS SURE that he hadn't heard her correctly. He was having a hard time hearing at all, since his blood was still roaring through his ears and his heartbeat was louder in his head than any sound in the room.

And yet he had heard it.

She had agreed to marry him.

And for some reason, instead of feeling like all the pieces were falling into place, he felt a bit like he was falling apart.

"I am glad to hear that, Rachel," he said.

"It seems like a weird conversation to have right now."

"No, I think a man should be flattered if a woman decides, after sex, that she will in fact marry him. Better than last time. After which you told me you didn't want to talk about it and stormed off."

She cleared her throat. "Um…it's just…all very confusing."

He shifted, holding her soft, curvy body against his. He put his hand on her stomach, as he'd done that night two weeks ago. It was still flat. No sign yet of the baby she carried. If it weren't for the scan earlier, he would hardly believe she was pregnant.

"And now it isn't? What changed your mind?"

"If I say the orgasm will you run away?"

He could have laughed at her candor—if his chest didn't feel like it had a pile of bricks on it. "No."

"Well, it wasn't that. Not really. But it is partly this. I can't imagine trying to raise a child with you. Seeing you. And having it not be like this and I thought… I just thought, and I'll be perfectly honest with you, how if I didn't marry you there would be other women. That you might have a child with someone else. I don't want that, Alex. Which brings me to the next part—if you marry me, I'm the only woman you get."

Her demand warmed him in a strange way. That she could be jealous. That she would want to ensure only she had him. "That's just fine with me."

"Really?"

"Yes. I have no desire to ever make you feel used. And it's not just because of your past, but because of mine. Of my mother's."

"You loved her, didn't you?" she asked.

Her words hit like an arrow. "Yes," he said. "She was my mother."

"But a lot of people would be angry with their mothers for putting them in that position."

"She was a victim, Rachel. Nothing more. Sad and utterly pathetic, and I do not have it in me to be angry with her. No one on all the earth loved her but me, and I am happy to be the one who did. The one who does." The words stuck in his throat, a note of sadness in them that he despised. Still the boy who longed for her love. The boy who'd never really had it.

"My mother… When she found out about the video—" she let out a shaking breath "—my dad had to tell her because it cost so much to pay off Colin. Mind you, they had a lot of money and she never would have noticed, but he felt like it was right. She was so ashamed of me. She'd taught me better, not to let men talk me into things. Never drink, never smoke, never tarnish our reputation. She'd told me to save my virtue. And I didn't, in her eyes. I embarrassed the whole family, ruined myself forever, and it would have all been avoided if I had just been…"

"More like her." He felt a lead weight settle in his stomach. So very strange, but he felt for her. Felt her pain. Just as he felt her pleasure when they made love.

"Yes. But you…you remember your mother's flaws and you love her."

"I do," he said, his throat tightening.

"I love mine, but sometimes I think remembering her as anything but perfect, the way everyone else seems to remember her, is an insult to her memory. I'm the only one who had that relationship with her. It's almost like I knew someone different."

"They're your memories, Rachel. They aren't wrong. And you have a right to feel upset about them."

"You're better than a therapist, Alex. Of course, while dealing with all of these old issues you're giving me a set of new ones. Also, you've given me a lot of issues in general."

"Have I?" he asked. Her joke, which he was sure was only partly a joke, made him feel unspeakably tired. Made him feel like he was ruining something wonderful.

"Nothing serious," she said.

"No, just a baby and a husband. I'm not giving you anything too serious."

"Hey, one day at a time, right?"

"So your solution is not to think about it?"

"No, I think about it. Okay, I don't really. But I am right now. I did earlier."

"That was the source of your breakdown."

"I'm afraid. Because I know how badly even a good person can hurt their child. I'm afraid that I'm really not good enough. I'm afraid that I can't do it."

"You have to get some confidence," he said. "Because I was raised in a brothel and drug house and I'm pretty sure you're our child's best chance at normal."

"I don't know about that."

"You're as normal as they're going to get, anyway."

"Love fixes a lot of things," she said. "Look at how you feel about your mother."

"Love one way isn't enough," he said, his voice rough, the words he hated to voice more than anything out there in the open now.

"Of course she loved you, Alex," she said. "She probably just had a hard time showing it. Like my mother."

But his mother's words rang in his ears. The last words she'd ever spoken to him.

You ruined all of this for me! I kept you all this time for him! And now you've taken him from me. He's the only thing I love. He's the only reason I kept you all this time! Because I knew then he would let us stay! And now he wants me to go. I have nothing left!

Me, mama. You have me.

I don't want you, stupid boy! I never did. I would rather die than be without him.

"I'm sure that's all it was," he said, the words hollow, the vision of his mother making good on her threat fresh in his mind. "Everything will be fine."

And he knew he didn't believe any of what he'd just said.

She had to call home. It had been nearly two months since her aborted wedding, and still no one knew about her engagement to Alex, about the baby.

Ajax and Leah had gone through a lot of drama, which had resulted in Ajax calling her. That had been awkward.

But he'd only wanted to talk about Leah.

He loved her, which made Rachel feel good. About everything. Because Ajax and Leah were meant to be together, and now, now that Ajax had been able to confess his love, they were together.

And they were going to have a much better marriage than he and Rachel would have ever had.

So great for them, but now she had to cross the hurdle of her and Alex. Hiding out in his house. Taking occasional trips to Cannes together to check in on the expanding boutique.

The good thing was, it was successful, and Alana was considering opening up a second location. And Alex was advising Rachel on investing so she was looking into other businesses, as well. She was becoming a regular venture capitalist.

It was something she had a knack for, and she had the trust fund to start up. Plus it kept her mind off all the reality she had crushing down on her. And oh man, there was a lot of reality.

For starters, she was growing some real, serious feelings for Alex, and that was hard to deal with. It was scary, especially when so much about their future felt scary. Then there was the fact that no one knew what was going on. The fact that she would have to share.

Then there was the wedding business.

Another big wedding. Just a couple months after she'd ditched the original one. The whole thing made her feel a little weird.

Or a lot weird.

Still, she had a phone call to make.

She pulled up Leah's number in her contacts and pressed Call, taking a deep breath and sitting down on the couch.

"Hi, Leah," she said when her sister picked up.

"Rachel! I haven't talked to you in…too long."

"I know. I'm sorry, but I'm sort of working my stuff out, and I didn't really want to interrupt you working your stuff out."

Leah sighed. "Yes, there was stuff. It's good now, though. I love him, Rachel," there was a slight pause, "and that's partly why we haven't been as close as we should have been these past few years. Because I always loved him. That's my fault, not yours. It's hard to be close to someone when they have the man that you love."

"You loved him?"

"Always," she heard a catch in her sister's voice. "I've always loved him."

A tear slid down Rachel's cheek. It was so easy to cry these days. "I'm so glad you married him, Leah, because I didn't love him. I never did. And if I'd had any idea that you did…I would never have put us all through this."

"It worked out. More than worked out. I'm so happy with him."

"I'm just… I'm glad. I'm so glad."

"Okay, now you have to tell me about Alex, because I've been worried about you. We've been worried about you. Ajax, too."

Rachel smiled. "Yes, he would be. Of course."

"And Alex…he's Alexios Christofides."

Rachel hesitated. "He is."

"Did you know?"

She swallowed. "Not at first. But I did when I ran out of the wedding. I mean, that's the thing that I sort of need to tell you all." There was no easy or painless way to say it. So she just soldiered on. "I'm pregnant. Alex and I are having a baby."

"Oh… Oh, my gosh. I don't know what to say. I'll make you a candy bouquet for your shower."

Rachel laughed. "Oh, wow. Candy bouquet. Thank you. I don't…I don't think I want a shower, actually. I think I'm going crazy."

"Why?"

"Because it's not… He doesn't… He wants to marry me because of the baby. I said yes. I finally said yes because he's the father of my child and there's no other man I want to marry. So yes seemed like the thing to say. But now I've said it and it just feels… I'm scared. About all of it. Having a husband who doesn't love me. Having a baby when I can't remember the last time I held one."

"I can…see where that would be terrifying."

"Right?"

"And I know what it's like to marry a man knowing he doesn't love you. To have him look at you and know…and know it's not you he wants."

"Oh, Leah…"

Her sister paused for a moment. "If you don't want to marry him just come home."

"I think I do. Want to, I mean. I think I need to."

"Because of the baby? You don't, Rachel. We would all support you. You know that."

"I know," she looked down at her hands. Except she didn't know that. One more step out of line and she was finished. She was very likely finished already. "I do know that. I need to for me. Because as much as sometimes I feel like I don't know what I'm doing with him, I know I wouldn't be happy without him."

"That's the worst. I totally know how you feel."

"Ajax?"

"It's all good now," Leah said, sighing, "but at first… yeah. I had to make a choice. Did I want to be with him, even knowing that it wasn't going to be ideal, or did I want to be without him."

"And obviously you chose to be with him."

"Yes, and it worked out. But it doesn't always."

"I know that."

It was weird taking advice from her younger sister, but she badly needed it in a lot of ways. Because Leah was the authority on it, after all.

"I know you know, but someone has to say it. Just in case it got knocked out of your head by Alex's sweet, sweet loving, which, I'm assuming, is what drew you to him in the first place."

Rachel couldn't hold in the borderline hysterical giggle that bubbled up into her throat. "There is that. But you know…there was something else. From that first moment, there was something else."

She wasn't sure exactly what the something else was. And she was very sure she didn't want to know. Though she had a suspicion.

And like almost everything else involving Alex, it was the most exhilarating, terrifying thing she'd ever experienced.

"You love him," Leah said, in the knowing tone of someone who had been afflicted by the same thing.

Her heart sank, and a burst of joy popped inside of her at the same time. It was terrifying. And wonderful. And horrible. Suddenly it was like the walls had come down, and there was no New Rachel or Old Rachel or Rachel With the Walls of Steel Behind her Heart. There was just Rachel.

Rachel Holt, who loved Alexios Christofides more than anything. No matter what.

"Yes. I do. I love him."

"Hello, darling."

Alex walked into his bedroom, well, the bedroom he usually shared with Rachel, and stopped. She was standing there in nothing but a short lace nightgown, her expression nothing short of seductive.

"To what do I owe the pleasure?" he asked, undoing the top button on his shirt. He'd been conducting most of his business via Skype for the past couple of months, when possible, so even though he didn't leave the house, the video chats made it so he still had to dress up.

But he wasn't wearing a tie in his own home.

"Of what?"

"The seduction. Because that's clearly what's going on here."

"I told them. My sister, my father. About the baby."

He paused, squeezing tight on the button he'd been about to push through its hole, the blunt plastic edge biting into his finger. "And?" If they'd hurt her…if they'd said anything to her to make her feel like she'd dishonored them in some way…he feared his actions would be less than noble. Possibly less than legal.

Because Rachel was *his*. And no one was ever to hurt her.

"They were…surprisingly calm. But I think relieved because I explained why I did what I did. I mean, it's awkward having to say to your dad 'I met a man and I was overcome by attraction to him' but I managed. To be honest, I think he preferred it to 'Dad, I put the car in a ditch while I was drunk' or 'Dad, I gave some guy a BJ and he videoed it.'"

"I'm certain he did," Alex said, his throat tightening. He wished he could get his hands on the scumbag who'd done that to her, that was for sure.

But then he really *would* do something illegal.

"Yes, well…I feel like I can't worry anymore. About letting everyone down."

"Is that right?"

"Yes. I need to worry about me. And us. And the baby."

"Not so scared of the baby now?"

"Oh, no, terrified. Utterly terrified. But I feel a little bit more like I can breathe again. Actually, I feel like I can breathe for the first time in a long time. Because… Because if I really am okay—as I am, I mean—if I really don't just have to be a clone of my mother? Well then maybe I can focus on being a good mom because I won't be working so hard to keep my façade in place. Does that make sense?"

"As much sense as any of our issues make."

She laughed, so sweet and beautiful in a lace nightgown, blond hair spilling over her shoulder, a seductress. Giggling. There was something so perfect about it. Something so free.

He wanted to capture it, hold it forever.

But then…then she wouldn't be so free. Then she would be in a cage fashioned by him, rather than one built by Ajax or her father.

The thought unsettled him. And yet it didn't diminish the need to hold her to him. To claim her.

"I guess that's true. I mean, none of it makes sense to anyone but ourselves, right? In here, though—" she put her hand on her chest "—it's been the realest thing in my life. Trying to deal with that critical voice, trying to best it, to be better. While secretly dying of boredom. I haven't even been able to be myself inside. I haven't even had emotions that belonged to me because…I was told so often I was wrong."

"I let go of emotions because it was the safest thing." Except he hadn't let go of them, not truly. Anger, rage and that impotent longing of a young boy for some kind of affection…it was all still there. And he hated it.

Silence fell between them, the light in her eyes changed. She looked fierce. Angry. "You should never have been subjected to the things you saw. It makes me want… I want to go back and protect you and I can't. It hurts to know that I can't."

He felt like she'd reached straight into his chest, taken his heart in hand and squeezed tight. "I do not need protection."

"Maybe not now, but you did. I wish someone had done that. I think it's wonderful that you love your mother, in part because no one else did. But I wish, so much, that someone had stepped in and protected you."

"You…care about me, Rachel?" he asked. They were hard words to speak, and yet it was harder not to say them at all.

"More than that, Alex. I actually... I wanted to say—and I was going to wait until I had you all sex-sleepy, but—I love you."

Alex froze. "Say it again," he said.

They were the words he'd wanted from someone all of his life. Words that had never, not once, been directed at him. Not by his mother, not by his father, not by a lover. Now that he'd heard them he wasn't sure what they made him feel. It was something deep. Something hot and cold. Something that made him want to pick up a car and throw it into the ocean, or just pull her into his arms and kiss the hell out of her.

Instead he waited, frozen inside. Even his heart had stopped. He was certain of it. Because he couldn't breathe, not at all. The world might even have stopped turning, just waiting, on pause, for the next words that might come out of her mouth.

"I love you."

She said it again, and it all started again. His heart pounding hard, causing a shift inside of him that made him feel like he was crumbling, each beat compromising the stone walls built up around him for protection.

He couldn't think of what to say. Or what to do. And that rarely happened to him. When it did, though, Rachel Holt seemed to be the cause of it.

"Why?" he asked.

He hadn't meant to ask the question, but the minute he did, he realized it was the word pounding through his head. Because it made no sense. Because no one ever had. And he wasn't sure why this beautiful, incredible, ridiculous woman who seemed to light the world on fire when she smiled, would feel that way about him.

Not when he'd used her. Seduced her for revenge.

"Because I cried in front of you. I want to seduce you, and be seduced by you, and say dirty words for you. I can sing off-key in front of you. And you don't judge me, or look down on me. You accept me that way, and I feel like I can accept myself that way, too."

"Is that all?"

"Achieving self-acceptance isn't big enough for you? Fine, that's not all. The sex is good, too."

He didn't feel torn about what to do anymore. He crossed the room and pulled her into his arms, kissed her until neither of them could breathe. Until his lungs were filled with her. Her scent. Everything.

Until his blood was so hot with lust he thought it would scald him inside.

He felt wild. Out of control. Unequipped to accept what she'd given him and unable to return it.

But one thing he knew for certain was that she was his. Love would make her stay. He'd truly done it. He had made her love him, and now that she did, she wouldn't go.

He'd seen that growing up. He'd seen it with his parents.

She would stay. His Rachel would stay.

He felt the need, the intense, unendurable need, to brand her and solidify that bond. Vows. Legal documents. He needed that marriage now. Needed to strengthen his hold.

Because she couldn't leave him. He couldn't lose her.

"Show me how much you love me," he said, his voice a growl he didn't recognize. The feelings in him utterly foreign, something that was also beyond his recognition.

"How?" she asked.

"Show me," he repeated, feeling desperate.

She pushed his shirt from his shoulders and kissed his neck, his chest, her fingers working at his belt, and the closure of his pants. Soon she had him naked, soft hands skimming over his body.

He just wanted to drown in it all. In her touch. In the moment. To never have this moment pass so that he could live in it forever.

But it was already passing, changing. And he couldn't regret it because of where it put her hands. The way that she cupped him. Squeezed him. Teased him. Her hands sure on his body, her lips soft, her tongue hot and slick.

She moved away from him and a kick of fire burst through him. Her not touching him was going to drive him insane, but he had to let her stop, because he had to see what she would do next.

He was powerless to do anything but watch her.

She took the lacy nightie off, exposed her body to him slowly. And in her eyes he saw her emotions. She wasn't pausing to make jokes. Wasn't interrupting the moment, the tension, with a comment.

It was the first time she'd simply met his eyes and taken her clothes off.

He was glad she wasn't talking because he was sure he couldn't have spoken if he'd wanted to.

She returned to him, full breasts pressed against his chest. He pushed his thigh between her legs, felt her wetness on his skin. Her desire for him.

He put his hand on her lower back and rocked against her. Her head fell back, lush lips parted, a sweet sound of pleasure escaping her mouth.

He cupped her chin, held her steady, bending to kiss her as he continued to move, continued to pleasure her.

He would give her this. Not love. But this. And she loved him, so it would be enough. Because she'd said he made her feel good. And that the sex mattered.

He would show her just how good he could make her feel. Just how much sex mattered. He would give her everything that he had to give. Everything.

He slipped his thigh from between her legs and walked her backward to the bed, pushing her down so that her butt was resting on the mattress and her legs were over the side.

"I need you," he said, the words painful to force out. "You don't know how much."

He hooked her legs over his hips and thrust into her. Her back bowed off of the bed, her round breasts thrust into prominence. He took one nipple in his mouth and sucked it in deep, until she moaned. Until he felt her internal muscles tighten around his cock.

She grabbed his shoulders, her fingernails digging into his back as he thrust into her, hard and uncontrolled. He didn't have it in him to be measured. Wasn't able to take his time.

He needed her too badly. He needed to keep going, to run from the roar of blood in his ears, to push toward a release that would make the ache in his chest go away. That would make everything clear and calm. An orgasm to purge him of all the longing and pain that were weighing him down.

He gripped her hips, tugged her to meet his body with each movement. He couldn't get enough. He didn't think he ever would. He'd never felt like this before. Like he was unraveling at the seams.

She cried out her release and it pushed him over the edge, his climax engulfing him as he leaned forward, hands braced on the mattress on either side of her as he shuddered out his release. His muscles were shaking, his body trembling. It had been the most intense sexual experience of his life.

But it hadn't taken away the weight. The pain. The confusion.

But it had left one thing deeply rooted in him. She was his.

He moved away from her, lay down on the bed beside her, his legs off the edge like hers, as he tried to catch his breath.

"I will plan the wedding for as soon as it can possibly be coordinated," he said.

"What?"

He looked over at her, watched her breathe hard. It was rewarding when she was topless. And yes, even with all of his inner turmoil he appreciated the gentle motion of her breasts. Or perhaps, because of the inner turmoil, he appreciated it particularly.

"The wedding. There is no point in putting it off. Your pregnancy is going to become evident soon." He put his hands on her stomach, it was a bit fuller than the last time he'd done that. A strange surge of pride shot through him, one he didn't want to examine too closely.

"Maybe I like the maternity bride look."

"Do you really?"

"No."

"Okay then, since you've made the decision. And since you love me...I see no reason to put it off."

"You're high-handed."

"Yes."

"You're the younger man. You're supposed to be my boy toy, but you're all alpha and stuff."

He rolled over and put his hands on either side of her, his chest touching her breasts. "You like it."

"I do."

"So don't complain. We will be married within the next couple of weeks. I'll hire a coordinator and you can submit all of your ideas to her."

"Well, that sounds...easy."

His heart seized up. "You have a complaint about it?"

"No, not at all. Not really. I already kind of just planned a wedding. For the entire last year of my life. And I ended up not going to it, so this is kind of... I don't really care what this one is like."

That hit him wrong. "You don't care what your wedding to me is like after you spent a year planning your wedding to Ajax?"

"Don't be that way. That's not what I meant. I'm just...
The wedding itself doesn't seem that important, all things
considered. It's what it means. It's what our lives will be
after."

"And what will our lives be?" he asked.

"We'll be together."

Yes, she was his. She truly was. His muscles relaxed,
his entire body getting the post-sex languor he'd been an-
ticipating.

There was nothing to worry about. He'd been in control of all of this, from beginning to end. Sure, things had
gone off the rails a couple of times, but in the end, he was
getting what he wanted.

In the end, he was getting her.

CHAPTER ELEVEN

IT WAS HER WEDDING DAY. Again. How strange to have a second wedding day in just over three months' time.

But here it was, that time again.

She smoothed down the front of her wedding gown and looked in the mirror. It was a simple chiffon dress that flowed over her stomach. Her stomach which was not up to being squeezed into anything fitted. It was tender and she was already having to ponder maternity pants.

The difference this time was that she loved Alex, and she knew that being with him was what she wanted. No, he didn't exactly love her back. Or at least he hadn't said that he did, but she wanted to be with him.

And as Leah had said, sometimes you had to make choices.

They were marrying on Alex's island, rather than her father's estate. It made her feel sort of wistful and sad. Actually, the fact that her family didn't feel as much a part of it as her first wedding made her feel wistful and sad.

And Alana hadn't been able to make it, either, because she was attending a movie premiere in the States, as the guest of a celebrity she'd dressed. Great for her, but sucky for Rachel. Not that she would have ever asked her friend to give the opportunity up.

It was for their business, after all. It was Alana's career, but it was Rachel's investment. It was a nice distraction, really. Knowing that was going on halfway around the world.

Weddings, whether she loved the groom or not, made her nervous, it turned out.

But at least she knew she wasn't going to have any past lovers crashing this one.

She took a deep breath and picked up her bouquet. No, nothing was going to mess this day up. And then she and Alex would be married and the rest would…just work itself out.

She ignored the leaded weight in her stomach that said otherwise.

Alex looked out his office window, down to the grounds below. Chairs had been set up by the water, and people were already filling them. An arch was in place at the altar. There were flowers all over it. It looked a little bit fussy for Rachel. Not any more indicative of who she was than the first wedding had been. But then, she'd said she didn't want to be part of the planning, so the coordinator had taken the helm.

She'd have to be happy with what she got, because she was the one who'd made the decision not to make decisions. And he shouldn't care if it "looked like Rachel" or not.

It didn't matter. All that mattered was that the wedding happened, and quickly.

It was all about to begin. It was, in fact, time for him to head down there. He opened the door and started down the hall.

This was it. The final piece to keep her with him.

Because she made him feel new. She made him feel like he was something other than his blood. She made him feel like a man who was loved.

And he needed that. He needed her.

He went down the stairs and threw open the front doors

of the mansion, striding down the walk and toward the beach. He made his way down the aisle, ignoring the head turns of the guests. People he didn't know. All of them were Rachel's guests.

Because no one was here for him. He brought nothing in terms of connections or friendships to the marriage. He had no friends. He had clients. He had enemies.

He had Rachel.

And that was all.

She had friends. She had a family who loved her. A lightness to her, that even with her pain and vulnerability seemed to shine through.

She was good. And that wasn't something that could ever be said about him. There was a reason no one had ever loved him.

A large rock settled in the pit of his stomach, growing heavier with each step. Making each step a challenge.

And as he stood there at the head of the aisle he scanned the crowd, and his eyes met with those of Ajax Kouros. Sitting in the front row, by himself, his wife likely gone to wait with Rachel.

Ajax looked very like their father. It was a blessing in Alex's mind that he himself did not.

He wondered if they looked very much like brothers to a disinterested party. He thought he might see some similarities. The same jaw. The same chin. Ajax's eyes were dark, while Alex had his mother's eyes.

But as he stood there, a sick, horrifying feeling washed over him.

Ajax had their father's eyes. Their father's love. A love that Alex shouldn't have wanted, but that he did want. Because he'd wanted someone's love. Anyone's. And Ajax had the love of so many. His wife, his father-in-law. He had a family. He had friends.

Alex was alone.

Alex, who was conniving to trap this woman, this loving beautiful woman, into a marriage that would offer her so very little.

The way his father had kept his mother in the compound. On a leash made of drug addiction and a terrifying, unhealthy love.

Alex was no better. He had used a woman's body in a bid for revenge. And now he was tying her to him when he knew he could give her nothing but his anger, nothing but the black, wicked blood in his veins.

As he saw Ajax sitting there, Alex saw nothing more than a man. Not a monster, not a demon.

No, the demon had never been in Ajax. The demon had always been within Alex. It was the thing he feared, the thing he hated. And it was him.

That was why no one loved him. Why his mother had taken death over a life with him.

It had always been him.

He took a step back down the aisle. And another. And another, until he was walking away from the beach, back toward the house.

He stumbled inside and closed both doors behind him. And he looked up and saw Rachel coming down the stairs, with her sister, Leah, trailing behind, helping with the train of her gown.

She looked like an angel. All in white, the gentle rounding of her stomach highlighted by the soft, flowing fabric. Her blond hair was in loose curls, a halo of gold that made him ache. Made him hate the man who had taken her innocence and used it in his games.

Hate himself. More than he had ever hated Ajax. More than he had ever hated his father.

More even than he'd hated his mother as he'd watched the blood drain from her body, as he'd watched her steal herself from him.

Why would anyone ever love the creature he was? His mother must have known, even then, what he was. She had been able to love Kouklakis, but she'd never been able to love Alex. Had killed herself rather than face life away from the compound. Rather than face a life with just herself and Alex.

If there was anything more telling he didn't know what it was.

I would have saved you. He'd wept that day. So hard. Without hope. *I would have given you everything.*

It had never mattered. Because he wasn't enough. He would never be enough.

"I need to talk to you," he said.

She blinked. "What about? Is everything okay?"

"We need to talk, Rachel."

"Okay. Leah, can you give us a moment?"

Her sister nodded and headed back up the stairs, giving him a hard look that let him know she wasn't overly impressed with him. Well, she would be even less impressed after this. But it didn't matter. None of it mattered. He had just had a look in the mirror for the first time, so to speak, and he'd confirmed what the deep, clawing ache in him had always hinted at. No one hated him more than he did.

Except for maybe Rachel. But she would hate him even more if he subjected her to a lifetime of him.

"I am not marrying you," he said.

"What?"

"You heard me," he said. "I am not marrying you today."

"Why the hell not? I have a dress. We have a marriage license. What in the world is wrong with you?"

"I have something I haven't told you. Something that will change the way you feel about me. It could do nothing else."

"What you just said has already started to change the way I feel about you."

"Understandably. And you need to hear this, too."

She threw her bouquet down on the step, spreading her arms wide then slapping her hands down on her hips before crossing her arms beneath her breasts. "All right. Great. Let's hear it. Come at me, bro."

"Ajax Kouros is my brother."

That shocked her silent for a moment. "Say what now?"

"Ajax is my brother. Nikola Kouklakis is our father. We have different mothers. I have never known who Ajax's mother was, and doubtless he didn't, either."

"Why didn't he ever say anything?"

"He doesn't know. I didn't find out until years after he'd left. He left when I was eight or so, he would have been… sixteen. He never knew." He swallowed hard. "When I was fourteen I was told who my father was, by Nikola himself. I was terrified, because I'd always been afraid of him. I'd always hated him. But, he said, with Ajax gone I would have to be his heir. And then… And then he told my mother it was time for her to go because she'd outlived her usefulness there. She'd provided me with…a mother's presence, I suppose, and now he no longer needed her."

Alex paused, his heart pounding, his body shaking. He'd never told anyone about this. Had never spoken these words out loud. He hated this memory. Hated this moment in his life. Hated this truth.

"He told me how he had cared for me. How he had forbidden any of the men in the house from touching me, both when I was a boy and when I was older. How he made sure I got fed. I always thought it was her. But it wasn't. It was never her." He took a deep breath, afraid he might throw up. "I ran out of his office. I wanted nothing to do with him. With all of it. She was so angry with me. She told me…I'd ruined everything. She never wanted me. It was all for him. Everything she'd done for me had always been for him. I told her I would take care of her. I told her it would be all right." Everything turned cold inside of him.

"What happened?"

"She killed herself. In front of me. Because that future, the end of everything, was preferable to a life spent with me."

Rachel's eyes widened with horror, her view of life already darker because of him. Because of his truth. He was ruining her already. "Alex...I don't... She had problems, Alex, it wasn't you."

"It wasn't me? She loved Nikola Kouklakis, and she couldn't love me. Everyone loves Ajax. He came out of it...fine, just fine. I'm broken. Everything in me is...I am his son. All of the bad things are in me. I cause...destruction just by breathing."

"Based on what? The actions of a woman who was too broken to know real love when she saw it?"

"It's more than that. It was what my father did—he broke people. And I do it without even trying."

"That's not true. I don't care who your father is. I don't care who your brother is. What your last name is, where you came from. If your mother was a prostitute or if *you* were a prostitute. I don't care. I know who you are now. I love who you are now."

Her words burned in him, a sharp, almost refreshing sting. Antiseptic on an infection. He couldn't accept it.

"You can't."

"I do. Alex, I love you. Your mother had a lot of things going wrong inside of her, and they weren't your fault. She couldn't love you, but that was because of her own heart, not yours. There's nothing broken in you. You're a good man, and I love you more than anything."

He couldn't take it. He couldn't. All he could see was his mother's face, so haunted and broken at the thought of life away from the compound. Life with him. And then lifeless and blank as she lay there dying.

He thought of Ajax, who'd transcended it all. Who'd

found love and a life away from all of that while it all seemed to cling to Alex like creeping slime.

It would never come clean. Ever. He would only poison her, too.

"Don't be so naive," he said. "It was always going to happen this way. I didn't want Holt. I never did. I wanted nothing less than your and Ajax's utter humiliation. His leaving is part of what triggered my mother's suicide. He escaped with no consequences, and it was my job to give them to him. Now he has married your sister, the second-choice bride, because he couldn't have you. And then, I'll make you available to him now that it's too late. Now that you're having my child and he's married to someone else. Don't you see how well you were played? Don't bore me with any more of your declarations of love. They mean nothing, because you don't know who I am. You can't love me," he said, the words choked. Because he knew they were true. She couldn't love him. "You can't love someone you've never truly met."

She raised a shaking hand, a tear sliding down her cheek. "Then it's nice to meet you, Alexios Christofides."

He extended his hand and closed his fingers around hers. She was so soft and perfect he wanted to weep. This was the last time he would ever touch her. She would leave him now, and it would be for the best. For her. For their child.

Their child should never know him. Everyone was better off without him in their lives.

"I'm sure you don't mean that," he said.

"No," she said, "actually it really sucks."

"Shall you tell them all it's off, or shall I?"

"I will," she said. "I can handle this myself. You've done enough. I'll send for my things later. We won't speak again. I assume you don't want anything to do with the baby?"

His heart screamed. And he ignored it. "No."

"Great. Great, that's just…great. If you come near my family again, I will castrate you, do you understand? Because you've liberated me, and I will not go quietly. I won't let you get away with *any*thing. If you show up in our circles, I swear I will have your head on a pike. You thought your revenge on Ajax was bad? Just wait." She walked past him and pushed the doors open, the sun illuminating her. She was no innocent angel now, she was an avenging angel. Caught on fire with the light of the sun. He had to look away. He closed his eyes and he could still see the impression of her behind his lids, burned there. He had a feeling when he closed his eyes it would always be her that he saw.

The doors closed. And he heard footsteps behind him.

And then something cold hit him in the back of the head. He turned and saw Rachel's bouquet on the floor behind him, damaged now beyond recognition from hitting him. And then there was Leah, standing there looking like she was ready to castrate him in the real world.

"It's not over for you," she said. "Not by a long shot. When Ajax finds out what you did…"

"Let him come. Tell him to bring all the firepower he has. I don't have anything to lose." Not now. There was nothing left for him to lose that had any value or meaning. He'd just cut ties with the woman he… The woman who meant more to him than he could ever say. And his child. A child he would never see. Never touch. Never hold.

It's for the best. It's for them.

He walked past Leah and went up the stairs, back toward his office. He walked into the room and slammed the door behind him, locking it.

He looked out the window and saw Rachel standing beneath the awful, ugly arch all alone, explaining to all those people that there would be no wedding.

Then the world tilted beneath his feet and he found himself on the floor, on his knees. He couldn't breathe. He didn't think he would ever be able to get back up because he was crushed under the weight of it all.

He had lost her. And it was only just now that he knew he loved her.

But it didn't matter. Loving her wasn't a kindness if it meant binding her to a man who was poison down to his core. Everything he'd done to her since they'd met... He was so bitter and twisted and she deserved more than that.

She deserved everything. She deserved someone who wasn't broken.

He'd been broken from day one. Somehow...fundamentally in a way that made it so no one could ever love him. A tool for his father, a pawn for his mother.

She deserved better. Rachel deserved everything.

Hot, wet tears were on his cheeks. He didn't care. He had caused Rachel's first tears in years, and now she had caused his.

A fitting end.

Theos, but he hated that it was the end.

CHAPTER TWELVE

"MORE CANDY, RACH?"

"Yes," Rachel moaned, holding her hand out to her sister and letting her fill it with little chocolate shoes.

She was lying on the couch in Leah and Ajax's penthouse in New York, where she'd been staying for almost two weeks trying to heal from a completely shattered heart.

She'd had a rage high for the first week. A total, deep and loathing hatred for Alex that made it impossible to cry over losing him. Made it impossible to think about their last conversation in any detail that went beyond the horrible, awful things he'd said.

She'd let it fuel her, carry her, keep her from collapsing.

In front of the wedding guests, she'd done nothing to take the high road. She'd done nothing to keep them from finding out what a hideous worm he was. She had been angry.

A mother bear, feeling rage for her cub. He'd said he didn't want to see their baby. His rejection of her was bad enough, but that rejection had opened up a well of maternal emotion she'd never felt before. It had given her a momentary, honest-to-God, deep desire to hurt him. Physically. To hit him with something hard. Repeatedly.

But now the rage had subsided. And parts of their final conversation were replaying, sections she'd tried to forget. His revelations about himself. How he felt about himself.

That his mother had killed herself rather than be with him. That the underlying tone of it all was that he was a man who felt unworthy. Of everything. He had hated Ajax, because Ajax had the one thing Alex didn't think he would ever truly be able to have.

Love.

And for some reason, her love hadn't been enough. Or, maybe, he was just afraid that her loving him would hurt her somehow.

And that made it harder to rage at him.

Something had happened at the wedding. She was getting surer and surer about it. But until she figured out what to do, until she had the energy to tell Ajax that Alex was his half brother, she was going to lie around and eat more of her sister's candy.

"You okay?" Leah asked.

"No. I don't know if I'll ever be okay. I think I love him still."

"Yeah, I know how that goes. It's the worst."

Ajax walked into the room then, looking handsome, as he always did, in dark slacks and a white shirt. She could see it now that she looked at him—his vague resemblance to Alex. But he didn't have those eyes. Or that wicked sparkle.

Well, he did a little bit when he looked at Leah. And that made her happy. Because this was, by far, the happiest and most carefree she'd ever seen Ajax.

"What's the worst?"

"*You* were," Leah said. "You know, when we almost got divorced."

"Yes," he agreed, his tone overly serious. Typical Ajax. "I was the worst."

"Hey, Jax," Rachel said.

"Yes?"

"Did you say anything to Alex at the wedding?"

"No," he said, frowning. "But you have to know, I never trusted him. I'm sadly not surprised by the outcome."

"But I am. I spent months with him. I was… He was my lover. We're having a baby. I felt like I knew him better than that and none of this really makes sense to me. So maybe he was that good of an actor. Or maybe there's a little more to all of this than it seems. So I thought I would ask."

"He didn't say anything. He…looked at me, but unless he has some sort of unrequited longing for *me,* I don't see how that's valid."

"Yeah, that's not his problem. Trust me."

She laid her head back down on the couch.

"Another movie?" Leah asked, her tone pitying. Good. Rachel deserved pity. She was alone. And with child.

"Yes. And cake. Is there cake?"

Ajax gave her a look that mirrored his wife's. "I'll get you some."

She took a deep breath and stared at the TV, not really absorbing what was happening. She was miserable. She was in love with a man who didn't deserve her love. A man who needed love like a flower in the desert needed water.

Alex was drying up inside. Dying. And he wouldn't get help. He was determined to embrace all that anger and push everyone who cared about him away.

And yeah, he'd really messed her life up and it felt horrible. But he'd done some good things for her, too. And maybe rather than melting she should try and remember it.

She put her thumbnail in her mouth and started gnawing on it. "You know, Leah, I don't really want to watch a movie."

"Do you still want cake?"

"Yes, oh yes, I want cake."

"Good. Cake you shall have. What do you want to do?"

"Talk maybe?" Rachel asked. "I think...I think we spent too many years not talking."

"My fault, Rach, really," Leah said, frowning. "I was lusting after your man. That made things hard."

Rachel shook her head. "Sure, there's that. But...if we were closer, wouldn't I have noticed?"

"I don't know. But I'm not in the mood to blame you for it. Anyway, Ajax and I worked out. So it's fine."

"I was supposed to make sure I wasn't a bad influence on you, you know."

Leah laughed. "You? A bad influence on me? You're so sweet and...sweet. And I'm not. Never have been."

"Well, I wasn't for a while." She thought of drunk nights in clubs. Driving too fast. "I was a pretty big partier for a while. But you were a kid. You wouldn't remember. Dad was always on hand to cover up for me. Mom was always on hand to disapprove."

"You had a secret life!" Leah said. "I'm truly impressed."

"Don't be. I was an idiot. See, this is why they wouldn't let me tell you! You're easily influenced."

Leah laughed again and Rachel couldn't help laughing in return, until she was almost breathless with it, the need for something other than sadness and anger taking over and hijacking her emotions until she was almost in hysterics.

Leah followed suit until they'd both slid to the floor, laughing. Over nothing and everything. Rachel wiped her eyes and looked at her sister, another giggle surging through her.

"I guess if I can laugh for a little bit... Hey, it's a start, right?"

Leah cleared her throat. "Yeah, Rach, it's a start."

Rachel smiled, a feeble attempt. Yes, it was a start. But she had a feeling the road to getting over Alex was longer than she could possibly imagine. She had a feeling the wounds would get cut open, raw and fresh again every time she looked at their child.

Especially if that child ended up with those beautiful, wicked blue eyes...

She hoped they wouldn't. And she hoped they would.

For now she would take a couple hours of distraction. Her broken heart was going to take a long time to heal, but at least she had her sister. She could spend some time with Leah, doing her best to forget her pain.

Alex hated having to get dressed. Lying around his apartment, drunk and in his underwear, was about his speed lately. But here he was, shaven and showered and wearing a suit. Because he had business to see to.

Business that involved a man who would very likely kill him on sight. But at least then there would be an end to the hell he'd been living in. Death seemed like a pretty serene option, all things considered.

"Mr. Christofides." A man who was sitting behind a large desk in the ante chamber of Ajax's office addressed him. "Mr. Kouros will see you now."

"Oh, good. I don't suppose you know whether or not he's in a killing mood."

"At work, Mr. Kouros usually is."

"Well," Alex said. "Damn." He forced a smile and walked toward Ajax's office.

"Alexios," Ajax said when he walked in. "I was surprised when you said you wanted to see me, and you made it necessary for me to dodge my wife's questions because I didn't want to upset her.... Anyway, you've put me in a bad frame of mind already so if I were you, I would speak quickly. If you've come to make some sort of arch villain monologue, you're wasting your breath. I don't care."

"Hardly. I thought you might want an explanation. For everything. For why I was after your company. After you."

"You were at the compound, weren't you?" Ajax asked, sounding weary, a tired look in his eyes. Yes, Ajax felt very much like Alex did about the whole business. "In which case I understand why you might have reason to dislike me. However, you should know, and I say this not to try and absolve me of sins past but so you have some closure, I was the key part in having my father's crime ring brought down."

"I am happy to know that. To know that you were a part of stopping it. I wish I had been."

"You're young," Ajax said. "It took me time and age to do the right thing."

"I was at the compound," Alex said. "But that's not really the important part of the story. The important part is what I found out after you left."

"And what is that?"

"Your father had another son."

"That doesn't surprise me," Ajax said, though some of the color had leeched from his face.

"Well, it did me. Knocked me on my ass, in fact."

"And why," Ajax asked, his voice rough, "is that?"

"Because it's me."

Ajax paused. "You're sure?"

"*He* was. Enough to offer me his twisted kingdom when he passed, so I would say he was fairly certain."

"And that's why you've been after me? And my business?"

"I guess so. I was just blindly angry for the most part. How could you have escaped? And you had this perfect life. A family who loved you. A woman who loved you. And I had nothing. So I wanted to take it from you. Bring you down to the level I felt you should be on. The level I was on. But now I've hurt Rachel. And I'm not happy about that. I've also had a look at my own bloody self and let me tell you, it's not pretty. Rachel aside, I needed to speak with you about this. To let you know I'm not going to be pulling any more stupid stunts in the name of revenge. I'm tired. Tired of this. Tired of all the ugliness inside of me. I just want to let it go. And I'll never be the man she needs, I understand that. But I want to feel something other than… all of this anger."

Ajax grabbed a cup on his desk and straightened it, his knuckles white, because he was squeezing it too hard. "You understand, though, that because of Rachel, our relationship can't be…"

"I do. I don't think I'm the sort of man who has close family ties. At least, I don't know how."

Ajax looked down, his expression blank. "I am glad you told me."

"No more secrets. That old bastard doesn't get to have any of us anymore. No more power."

Ajax nodded slowly. "Yes. No more."

"Thank you for seeing me. This is hardly the kind of news you leave on a voice mail."

"Indeed not."

"I'll see myself out." He turned his back on Ajax and headed toward the door. Then paused, before turning back around. "Ajax, can I ask you a question?"

"Anything."

"How did you do it?"

"What?"

"How did you let it all go? How did you… How did you find it in you to ask a woman to tie herself to you for the rest of your life knowing where you came from? Knowing what's inside of us…how do you ever truly believe you'll rise above it? How can you ever believe you…deserve it when… No one has ever loved me. And I figure there's a reason for that. How do I tell her I want it when I'm afraid it will destroy her?"

Ajax was silent for a long moment, his dark brows drawn together, his focus out the window. Finally he spoke.

"Whatever our father said, whatever words he might have used, in my mind there was one thing he never did. One thing that he was missing that, had it ever taken root, would have changed the way he lived his life."

"And what is that?"

"He didn't have love, Alex. I think that's the thing that changes us. It's the only thing, at least in my experience, that can banish the monster."

"Love is what made my mother kill herself," he said, his tone flat.

"What do drugs do to you, Alex?" Ajax asked.

"They're addicting."

"They make you feel things," Ajax said, meeting his eyes now. "They make you need them. But you don't love them. They ruin you, make you think you can't live without them. Addiction isn't love. Which do you think your mother really felt for our father?"

Alex almost choked. "I…I'm not certain."

"Love is the thing that changed me," he said. "From Joseph Holt, to Leah, love was what truly healed me. It wasn't money or power. It wasn't vengeance. I didn't deserve it, either, but when I accepted it…that was when I changed. Think about it. Think about what love really is."

"I will."

"I hope you do. I really mean that."

Alex walked out of the office and down the hall, numb as he stepped into the elevator. Love. He was in love. A lot of good it did anyone.

He let out a roar of frustration and hit his fist on the button panel of the elevator, swearing roundly when it lit up several more buttons that signaled he would be taking a few more stops than he wanted on his way down to the lobby.

He leaned back against the wall, his heart pounding so hard he thought he might be having a medical crisis.

Was it so simple? Just loving and trusting that love

would make it all right? That it would bring forgiveness for everything that had happened? That it would stay? Could he truly have it, finally? The thing he'd craved his whole life?

Was it so simple to just say, "I love you, and I'm a mess and you deserve better? But please love me anyway"?

Would love light the way and keep him from going back into darkness? Would it make him a man deserving of that perfect, beautiful woman?

He pictured Rachel's face. Her beautiful smile.

Yes. Dammit. Yes. It would be enough.

He would never be worthy of her. Ever. She deserved a man who was whole. A man who would never dream of seducing a woman to get revenge on an enemy.

He wasn't that man. But he would let her cry, let her feel, and he would listen to her sing off key. He would hold her close at night and he would change their baby's diapers, because he wanted to be with her, and to share everything in this new, amazing life that he'd never once imagined he might have.

The elevator stopped. Fifth floor, of all the stupid things.

Then it stopped again.

And again.

Finally he was at the lobby, and by the time he was out on the street, he was sprinting. He was going to get Rachel. And he would beg if he had to.

But he had to take a chance.

Otherwise, all of his houses, his island, every cent of his money, wouldn't matter. Gaining all the world didn't matter if he lost the one thing he truly needed.

"Where is your dang ice cream, Leah Kouros?" Rachel muttered, rummaging through the freezer. "Why does your stupid candy company not make ice cream?" Unfortunately, her sister was down at Leah's Lollies today and was not in the apartment to hear Rachel cursing her name over her lack of frozen treats.

The front door opened and Rachel straightened. Maybe her angry mutterings had summoned Leah.

"I'm in here! How is it you have all this sugar and no ice cream? Answer me that."

"I don't know."

She turned around and dropped the spoon she was holding. It clattered on the tile floor, the sound ringing through the silence.

"Alex," she breathed. She felt like she was going to fall over. Felt like she'd been sucker punched. She hadn't seen him in nearly a month.

She put her hand on her stomach. Five months in and she was definitely looking her condition these days. "What are you doing here?"

His eyes dropped to where her hand was resting, a strange expression on his face. "Your body has changed."

"I'm pregnant," she said, "that happens. Especially since things are going well."

"They are?"

"Yes."

He let out a long breath. "I am relieved to hear it. Beyond relieved."

"I didn't think you cared."

"I'm a liar," he said, his words rough. "I care...Rachel, I mourn the changes in your body that I've missed. That it happened without me here. I should have been with you all this time. I should have been here. I should have...I should have been your husband."

"It was your choice not to be," she said, bending to pick up the spoon. "You were the one who walked back down the aisle and left me to explain why there wasn't going to be a wedding." She slammed the spoon onto the counter. "You made that decision. And then you told me it was your plan from the beginning. To use me. Because I was just a pawn to you. A pawn like I've been to everyone else. Except this was worse because with you I was honest. I told you how I felt, Alex. I showed you who I was and you took that and you abused it."

"I lied to you," he said.

"You what?"

"I lied to you because… Rachel, I got up there and I looked out in the crowd and I saw Ajax sitting there. And I knew…I hated him so much because of who I thought he was, but for some reason being up there and seeing him, my brother, made me see myself clearly for the first time. I hated what I saw. A man who used you. A man who contrived to trap you with him, even when he knew he had no hope of ever being all the things you deserved. A man who would hold you to him using any means, even your love against you. I saw myself in that moment. I saw that I was a man whose own mother couldn't love him and that she was right not to. I—" He took a deep, shaking breath. "I couldn't allow you to go through with it. Because everything that happened between us was so manipulated by me. Including your feelings. You say you love me…but that's because you're having my baby. Because you spent a few idyllic months on a private island with me."

She was sure that the room was spinning.

"Alex," she said, her voice trembling. "Are you telling me that you were acting the whole time we were on your island?"

"No," he said, "but it was so engineered, all of it. You felt trapped. I made you decide to come with me so quickly I…"

"Do you trust that I'm a smart woman, Alex?"

"Yes."

"Great. No hesitation even. So do you trust me to know my own heart?"

"Why? I sure as hell didn't know mine."

She frowned. "Poor man. Well, I know mine. I loved you. So much. And when you pushed me away...when you told me you never even wanted to see our child? I wanted to hit you with something heavy and blunt."

"That seems fair."

"I gave you my love, you...you jerk. I gave you everything. I would have—"

He pulled her into his arms and kissed her, deep, desperate. And she didn't push him away. Didn't fight him. Because she was too hungry for him. Angry, yes, she was angry. But she'd never stopped wanting him. She'd never stopped loving him.

He pushed her back up against the fridge, his hands on her waist as he kissed her. She wrapped her arms around his neck, tears streaming down her cheeks as she poured all of her hurt, all of her weeks of anguish into the kiss.

"Okay," she said, gasping for air, "we have to talk and not just have sex. The sex is fine between us. *We,* on the other hand, have problems."

"True," he said, breathing heavy.

"So why are you here?"

"Because I have spent the past month drunk and miserable. Because every time I think about never seeing our baby I want to die. And every time I think about never seeing you again...Rachel, I start praying for death to come quickly."

"Why?" she asked, her throat tight.

"Because I love you. With every broken, miserable piece of myself. And I realized this weeks ago but I kept thinking it wasn't fair to ask you to spend the rest of your life with a man like me. But...but I have to be selfish now and ask that you do. That you spend your life with me because if you don't then I'm not sure what my life means at all."

"Alex, why do you think you aren't worthy of me?" she asked. "I am... I'm not perfect. And I've fought to get to the place where I could say that and just be okay with it.

I'm not perfect. I've made mistakes. And I'll make more mistakes. I don't want a perfect man because I could never live up to those standards."

"I would give you a better man," he said.

"With all due respect," she said, "you're a jackass."

"Why?"

"Because I know what I need. I know who I am. I don't need better. There isn't better for me. For me, there's you. That's it. Alex, the moment I saw you I fell in love with you. Is that crazy? I would have thought it was crazy until five months ago when I saw you standing there, on a yacht. And you made me want things I never knew I needed."

He pulled her to him, crushed her against him, taking a sharp breath. "Me, too. Rachel, that was the moment for me, too. When you were standing there looking at me, so awkward and obviously attracted."

"Hey."

"It's true. You were. But it's okay, because that was the moment. When I knew that I needed you. I didn't know then that I needed you forever. I thought an hour. A night. I didn't know how much it would change me. But it did. And then you kept changing me these last few months. Even when you weren't there. Even when all that was left of you was how much I missed you."

"Why did it take you so long?" she asked. "Why did it take this long for you to know you loved me?"

"It was the one thing I'd never had before. I loved my mother, Rachel, but I didn't know what it was like to have her love me back. Not really. I didn't understand love as a living thing. As something that could give. She took. I gave. And in the end I was left devastated because…she ended herself rather than be with me, Rachel."

"Alex…it wasn't you. She had so many problems, honey, but they weren't you."

"I know," he said. "I do now."

"I'm glad. I'm so glad."

"Ajax helped me with that. He…he made me see. I hated him for what he had, without trying to find out why he'd been able to get it. Love. And when he told me that…it all made sense. Love is different than I thought. The love I feel for you has demanded that I change, that I give, that I sacrifice. And it makes me burn. Makes me want. Makes me hurt. Makes me so happy I… It's happiness like I never thought I could have. I had no idea what to call it, no idea what to do with it. It's love. And it's the most terrifying, wonderful thing I've ever felt before. And if you feel the same for me, if you want to do this—for the rest of our lives, knowing who I am, where I've been—then I can only be grateful. I can only try and become the man I think you deserve."

"Just be the man you are, Alex. That's the beginning and end of all I want from you. Because it's the freedom you gave to me. And it might seem like a small thing but… Alex, don't you see that you set me free? I feel like I was trapped in someone else's body, desperately trying to live up to an ideal I didn't even want to be and afraid I was failing miserably at it. You are… You are amazing. What you've given me is amazing. There is no better man to me than the man who simply wants me. As I am."

"I am that man," he said, kissing her cheek. "That I promise you. I want all that you are. All that you will be. We'll both keep changing, but we'll change together. Whatever life has in store for us, I think we can meet the challenge head on, as long as we're together."

"I think so, too."

"So, when are we getting married?"

"Not for at least six months," she said.

"What?"

"I need time to plan it. I love you and this is for life. And you love me. This is a real wedding. Also, I *don't* dig the pregnant bride look, I've decided."

"You're going to make me wait, Rachel?"

She smiled, her heart swelling. "For some things, Alex. Not for others."

A long time later they lay in her bed, limbs tangled, breathing hard. She was tracing his biceps with her fingertips, a smile on his lips. Yes, she loved this man, more than anything. Their start had been rocky at best, but they had forever ahead of them.

"You know, if we can make it through all of this, I think we can make it through anything," she said.

"I agree."

"Just as long as we're honest, from now on."

"In the interest of honesty then," he said, "may I say, I think your breasts have gotten larger. I like it."

"Wow. Romantic."

"Maybe not. But honest."

"Appreciated."

Suddenly, she flashed back to that evening they'd eaten pizza in a fancy hotel in Cannes. When he'd talked about happy endings. "You got your happy ending," she whispered.

He kissed her on the cheek and she could have sworn he left a teardrop behind. "It's not over yet."

"No," she said, snuggling closer. "It's not. And thank God for that."

"Yes. I get a whole lifetime with you. With ups and downs, with every emotion. But it will be with you."

She kissed his forearm and held his arms more tightly to her. "That's much better than any old happy ending."

He sighed, and she could hear the smile in his voice. "I agree, *agape*. I agree."

EPILOGUE

"It was a beautiful wedding," Leah said.

"And it *happened,*" Ajax added.

"You're sensitive as a blunt instrument," Leah said, beaming at her husband.

Ajax shrugged and turned to face Alex, who was standing there in a tux, his tie undone, his two-month-old son wrapped in a blanket and nestled in his arms. "Am I insensitive, little brother?"

Alex shrugged and looked down at his son. Liam didn't care that his parents had just gotten married. He was at peace, as he always was, everything in his world right. Alex's heart swelled with love, with pride. That his son had so much family to love him. That his life would be so much more beautiful than his or Ajax's had ever been.

That he would never know the harsh criticism of a mother the way that Rachel had. Never feel like he had to rebel or close up completely, rather than being who he wanted. That he would never wonder if he was loved at all. They told him every day.

"Yes, but it's part of your charm."

"Don't encourage him, Alex," Leah said.

Rachel returned then, on her father's arm. They had just finished their dance and Rachel was beaming. Her figure was still fuller than it had been before giving birth, her cheeks round. He loved it.

"How nice," Joseph Holt said, "to have all my children, and my grandson together in one place."

Alex's heart tightened as he looked around at his family. "Yes, it is," he said.

"Do you mind if I steal my grandson for a moment?" Joseph asked. "I'll trade you your bride for him."

"A deal."

He handed Liam to the older man, then took Rachel's hand, leading her out to the lit dance floor. "This wedding was much more you, wasn't it?" he asked, looking around at the simple décor. At the bright colors. It exuded joy. Just like his wife.

"Yes," she said. "But then, with you, I am much more me."

He kissed her nose. "I'm glad. I'm certainly a better me. It's amazing what can happen inside you when you start to understand love. When you replace anger with it."

"I'm glad you did, Alex, because you have so much love to give."

"I've never been as happy as I am today," he said, his wife in his arms, his son nearby.

"Then we have a new goal," she said.

"What is that?"

"To find even greater happiness, every day. As long as we live."

"With you, Rachel, that won't be hard at all."

* * * * *